First Flames

Fireside Romance Book 1

First Flames

Fireside Romance Book 1

by Drew Hunt

jms books

FIRESIDE ROMANCE BOOK 1: FIRST FLAMES

JMS Books LLC
10286 Staples Mill Rd. #221
Glen Allen, VA 23060
www.jms-books.com

Printed in the United States of America

ISBN: 978-1-46096-575-7

For everyone who craves sweet stories about love conquering all.

Chapter 1

MY LIFE, LIKE my job, was predictable, well ordered, and boring. However, the sameness was—for the most part—a comfort. When my alarm clock went off at half past seven each morning I could predict pretty accurately what I'd be doing that day. I also knew I would awaken alone when that alarm went off. That wasn't a comfort at all.

As I wandered along the library stacks pushing my trolley, putting returned library books back on the shelves, I thought about what life would be like if it were shared with another man. A man to come home to. A man to care about. A man who would care about me. A man to cuddle up with on the sofa of an evening, in front of a real fire.

Reaching up, I pulled out a copy of Grey's *Anatomy* which

someone had put with the astronomy books. I replaced it with a rather battered and ancient tome on the solar system. Here we were in 1986, and that book had been published before Neil Armstrong had stepped onto the moon.

A few months ago I'd taken the bus to Leeds—Leeds being the nearest large city—and gone into a gay bar. After being rejected a few times—once pretty painfully—what little confidence I'd had regarding the dating game evaporated.

Moving along the stacks I put the anatomy text book back in its rightful place.

All a potential mate would see when checking me out would be someone plain and ordinary. I was six feet even, had dark brown hair and washed-out green eyes. My face, not my best feature, was the big sticking point.

I sighed. This mythical potential mate could not see, or wouldn't take the time to find out what lay beneath the less than attractive exterior. If he did, he'd find someone with a big heart, someone who—if given a chance—would prove to be a fiercely loyal friend, who would put their happiness and feelings before his own. But, no, this book would most probably be judged by its cover. I grimaced inwardly at the bibliographical analogy.

The books safely returned to Dewey Decimal order, I pushed the empty trolley back to its place against the far wall.

Sinking into my chair behind the desk, I realised if my life were a book, it would be a bloody boring one. A title which would forever remain on the shelf.

Yes, I had low self-esteem. My confidence had pretty much reached rock bottom, and had purchased a pneumatic drill and was beginning to excavate. Unbidden, I let out a single bark of laughter. At least I had a reasonable sense of humour.

Mary—my colleague, best friend and confidante all rolled into one—rounded the corner and rested a hip against the desk. Unlike me, Mary was a really happy and out-going person who always had a laugh or a smile for me.

"Bloody hell, Simon, I'll be glad when this shift is over. My feet are killing me." She lifted her left ankle and gave it a rub.

"Well, my dear, you should have put on a sensible pair of shoes this morning, shouldn't you?" I said in my best aged-grandmother's voice.

She stuck out her tongue at me and immediately burst out into laughter.

"Shhh!" I said, then immediately joined her in laughter.

We often pretended to be stereotypical strict librarians, telling everyone to please remember they were in a hallowed place of study, so should conduct themselves with all due reverence. As expected, telling Mary to shush only served to make her laugh even more.

"Listen, love," she said, trying to be serious, "have you time for a cuppa at Daphne's after we knock off?" Daphne's was a cafe just a couple of doors down from the library.

"Sure." It wasn't as if I had anything else to fill my evening with. "My turn to buy the Eccles cakes."

Whenever I'd tried to make Eccles cakes myself, either the pastry didn't flake properly or the dried fruit oozed out of the slashes in the top. Daphne, or her supplier, did a much better job than I ever could.

"You'll have me putting weight on, ya know!" Mary exclaimed, rubbing her perfectly flat belly.

"All the better for me to hold you," I replied.

Mary was one of the few people who knew I was gay, and she 'didn't give a fig,' as she so eloquently put it.

"Sauce pot." She came around the desk. Bending, she whispered in my ear. "It's about time you found someone to hold."

"I know," I sighed. We'd had this conversation many times before.

Mary squeezed my arm in sympathy. Going back to the front of the desk, she looked over her shoulder at me. "It's a date then."

THE REST OF the afternoon passed with its usual mixture of students wanting a particular book and being disappointed to learn we either didn't have it or it was already out on loan. The Thatcher government had caused the local authority to cut back on spending on what they considered to be *non-essential* services. Libraries were a soft target and had received more than their fair share of the cutbacks.

I'd got rid of Fred, the town tramp who had occupied his usual place in the reading room nearest the radiator. He'd "just come in for a bit of a warm". He was harmless enough, and on the occasions when I'd had the time to sit and talk to him, I'd found him to be a fascinating source of information on the Second World War. He was one of the first troops to land in France on D-Day. He had lost his best pal, Henry, in that campaign. From how he spoke about him, I strongly suspected Fred and Henry had been more than just pals, but I never asked. From all accounts, Fred was never quite the same again after the war was over.

With the library empty of readers, Mary and I closed and locked the doors to the non-fiction section and went into the main office and signed out. Once that duty was done we interlocked our arms—as was our custom—and headed out of the library building and down the street to Daphne's.

WE FOUND OURSELVES at our usual table in the window, a pot of coffee between us. Neither Mary nor I liked the traditional English beverage of tea. We had also chosen our second favourite cake—cream doughnuts—all the Eccles cakes having been sold earlier.

From our vantage point looking out onto the high street, we were able to play our usual game of man-watching.

"He'd suit you right down to the ground," Mary said of one guy who had just come out of Boots the Chemist.

In truth the man did look kind of hunky in his black bomber jacket, the collar turned up against the cool evening.

"He's probably married," I sighed. "All the good ones usually are."

"Funny, I always found the good ones were all either married or gay, so that gives you a chance with at least half," Mary said, draining her cup.

Our other favourite game was to guess what a particular individual did for a living.

Mary's best guess that day was to whisper to me that one man—mid-forties but still quite fit looking—was a secret agent for the Russians. He masqueraded as a prostitute to get women into bed to learn their secret recipes. He'd pass this information back to the KGB. They would then take over the western world by developing the best tasting Yorkshire pudding and selling it at an ever increasing price. Thus they'd gain enough capital to be able to buy out all the multi-national companies of the world, and hold them under the yoke of the Soviets.

Did I mention Mary had a screw loose?

After we calmed ourselves down from that piece of outlandish deduction, Mary decided it was time she headed home. She still lived with her parents and dated occasionally, but hadn't found Mr Right, yet. I dated not at all, and of course I too was still looking for Mr Right. I had my own place about a fifteen-minute walk away. It was a rather basic two up, two down; all I could afford, but it was mine. Well, the building society's.

Mary's words of a few minutes earlier re-awoke something I'd been considering for a while. I'd thought about hiring a guy for a couple of hours. I didn't think I could go as far as actually having sex with him, but perhaps he'd agree to just sit and talk, or maybe we could have a kiss and a cuddle. I'd almost approached one of these men a few times, but had always chickened out at the last second.

After bidding Mary goodbye outside Daphne's, I squared my shoulders, set my jaw and ventured toward the back streets of our town and the red light district. Once on Gamble Street—the place where I knew a few rent boys plied their trade—I began to experience the same doubts I'd had before, but I pushed them aside and walked with the most confident manner I could muster, up to a young man of about nineteen or twenty years of age. He was wearing a faded black T-shirt which was a little on the small side for him, a pair of worn blue jeans, and white trainers. He was a couple of inches shorter than me with curly black hair. As I drew closer still I saw his eyes were grey-blue. He was good-looking, and under normal circumstances—say in a gay bar—I wouldn't have stood a chance.

"Hi, mate," he said in a low—and, to me, sexy—voice "What you after?" He had a faint but detectable Geordie accent. I thought it was…well…sexy.

Haltingly I asked, "Uh, what do you, um, offer?"

He smiled reassuringly. "Anything and everything, so long as we're safe."

"Um, would it be all right if we just went back to my house and uh," my voice, low to start with, whispered, "Just sat and cuddled and…" I knew my cheeks were flaming red. This was a bad idea.

The man's smile increased. "Sure, mate, not a problem."

After agreeing a price, I realised I'd actually committed myself, we walked the ten minutes or so to my place.

Although the temperatures were about average for early September, I thought a thin T-shirt didn't afford adequate protection, but that I guess was his business.

Conversation was a little forced on my part. We exchanged names, and he said I could call him Jim. I doubted if that was his real name, but that was his business.

We eventually arrived at my house. I unlocked the front door and ushered him in.

The front door opened into the main room.

"First things first," I said, getting out my money and paying Jim. I guessed it was usual to deal with such things at the beginning.

"Thanks." Jim tucked the notes into his front jeans pocket.

"Want a drink?" I offered beer, sherry. I could have kicked myself for that last. It seemed, well, inappropriate somehow.

"Do you have anything soft?"

"Diet Coke?"

"Perfect." Jim's smile was back. He was so handsome.

When I returned from the kitchen, can of Coke in hand, Jim was looking at my rather extensive video collection, which was shelved along one wall and all in alphabetical order—once a librarian, always a librarian.

"You've got a few nice titles 'ere, mate," he said.

"Would you like to watch one?" I asked.

I left him looking through the selection while I put a match to the fire I'd laid that morning. Although the house had gas central heating, I liked a real fire, and it wasn't cold enough to justify switching on the boiler. After the fire had taken hold, I looked up to see which film Jim had selected.

"*South Pacific* has always been one of my favourites."

I was a bit surprised; I thought he'd go for a James Bond, or some other action movie.

"It's one of my favourites, too." I smiled.

I put the tape in the machine and we settled down to watch. We began by sitting next to each other, but soon I lay across the back of the sofa. Jim settled himself in front of me, the top of his head under my chin. I slowly worked an arm under him, and put the other one over him, squeezing lightly. He gave out a quiet sigh.

My attention drifted from the screen to take in my surroundings. Dusk had fallen outside, and the only illumination in the darkened room came from the TV screen and the fire. I looked at the warm body next to me. Jim had moved further down my front, and I'd worked myself a little flatter, allowing

Jim to put his head on my shoulder. The situation began to tug on my emotions. I had lost count of the number of times I'd dreamed of such a scenario, someone warm and soft to cuddle up against in a cosy room, something romantic on the telly, all lit by a flickering fire. My eyes began to water at how nice everything looked and felt. I was able to block out the fact that the only reason this was happening was because I'd paid someone to help fulfil the fantasy. It just felt so nice…right…perfect.

A bleeping noise shook me out of my thoughts. I looked up at the clock on the mantelpiece and saw my two hours of bliss were about to come to an end. The noise must have come from Jim's watch. I made to get up.

"It's okay, I can stay longer if you like," Jim said in a quiet, almost sleepy voice.

"I'd love you to stay longer, but…a librarian doesn't earn all that much, and…" I raised my arm to let Jim free.

Jim twisted around before I'd had a chance to wipe away the tears that had fallen earlier.

"It's okay. I like it here. There's no extra charge." He lifted up on one elbow and gave me a quick peck on my lips. It felt wonderful. I put my arms back around him and managed to choke out through a quickly tightening throat, "Thanks, Jim."

"Please, call me Mark. I feel safer, a bit more removed from my customers, if I don't give them my real name. I like you, Simon, so I wanted you to know my real name."

"Thanks, Mark. I think I like you, too," I managed to get out through a throat that hadn't grown any less tight.

At that moment both our stomachs began to rumble. Mark let out a quiet chuckle. I did, too.

"Would you like something to eat?" I asked him.

Mark nodded. "If we can bring it back in here—and finish off the film. I've seen it so many times, but it's nice to watch it in such pleasant company."

I smiled. "I often have my tea in front of the telly. There isn't much point in setting out the dining table for just me."

I didn't have a dining room. Just a kitchen worktable with leaves that folded out to allow up to four people to sit round it. Not that I ever had that many guests.

We both got up and went into the kitchen to see what I could cobble together from what lay in the far corners of the fridge.

"There's a couple of chicken breasts, some tomatoes that are only fit for frying, and a bit of salad. Would these along with some pasta and a jar of pasta sauce do you?" I asked Mark.

"Great. Do you need a hand?"

"Thanks. If you could get the packet of pasta and the sauce from the pantry over there, that'd be a help."

We soon began to get the meal together. We seemed to work pretty well as a team. Domestic harmony, *Yeah right, Simon,* I thought to myself, *dream on!*

I cut the chicken into strips; Mark said it would cook quicker that way. I wasn't all that domesticated, I just knew enough to feed myself the basics. I didn't see the point in going to a great deal of trouble, when I was the only one who would eat the end results. I made a bit more of an effort on the few occasions when Mary would come over, but on the whole, I just did for myself.

The meal was soon ready. We went back into the living room where I got out a couple of TV dining tables, setting them up in front of the sofa. After we both got settled, I switched the VCR back on. We ate in cosy silence, with occasional comments from one or other of us about the food or the movie.

We'd pushed away the tables from the sofa, and I had my arms back around Mark when the final scenes came on, the ones where Liat, the native Island girl, finds out from Nellie that Joe Cable, the man Liat loved, had been killed in action.

"No matter how many times I watch this film, this bit always makes me cry," Mark said.

I agreed with him.

When the titles began to roll, I looked down at the tears on Mark's face.

I don't know where I got the courage, because I'd never done such a thing before, but I lightly kissed Mark's eyes. He gave a contented sigh of pleasure.

I pressed rewind on the VCR and got up to turn on the lights. It was totally dark outside now. The extra light in the room seemed to dispel the cosy mood. I knew Mark had to go soon, so I thought it better I bring up the subject. He'd been good enough to stay longer than we'd agreed, and I didn't want to impose on his generosity any further.

"I guess you'll have to make a move," I said.

"'Fraid so," he replied.

Walking over to the window to draw the curtains, I saw the glow of the streetlights reflected in the puddles on the roadway. It must have been raining steadily for a while.

I turned to Mark in his thin T-shirt. "You can't go out wearing just that. I've got a jumper and an old raincoat upstairs. Will you let me go get them for you?" Before Mark could object, I ploughed on. "I outgrew them, so they're no good to me…and you'd be doing me a favour by taking them and—"

"Thanks, mate. That's really nice of you."

I went upstairs and dug out the promised items. They fit him quite well.

"Thanks, Simon, these'll be a big help." I didn't really give much thought to his statement at the time, but after he'd gone I wondered if he had many clothes.

"I'd like to do it again sometime, but…" I looked down at my shoes, "I don't earn much so I can't say when."

Mark touched my cheek. "Looking forward to it."

We bade each other goodnight and I shut the front door and returned to my seat on the sofa. After looking at the discarded plates on the TV tables, I got up again and took them into the kitchen. While going through the usual domestic routines, I pondered on the evening's events. I wondered what Mark really thought of me. He couldn't have been too disgusted, as he'd agreed to stay longer than he had to. I imagined he occasionally got strange requests from his clients, so I didn't think mine would have been too weird for him.

Feeling a little tired after the day's events, I put the fireguard in front of the fire, turned off the lights and went upstairs to prepare for bed. Undressing in the bathroom prior to getting into the bath, I looked at myself in the mirror and thought, *You'd have stood no chance with Mark if we'd met socially.* The pneumatic drill was at work again, burrowing even deeper.

After a soak in the bath, I got out and dried myself. Stepping into a pair of boxer shorts, I stood at the sink and brushed my teeth.

Once in bed, I looked at the cover of the book I was reading, but decided I wasn't in the mood, so I switched off the bedside light and settled down to sleep.

Naturally my thoughts drifted back to Mark. I wondered what he was doing now. Would he have gone home, or to wherever he slept, or back to Gamble street to pick up another customer? I heard the rain splatter against the window, so hoped he'd gone home. I drifted off to sleep with thoughts of Mark's warm body that had—for a short time at least—been held next to mine.

Chapter 2

GETTING TO THE library at 8:30, I walked into the main office, signed in and generally went through the usual motions of starting the workday.

Mary breezed in just in time.

"You'll be caught out one of these days," I cautioned in my mock parental voice.

"I know, I know. I got chatting to the milkman and lost sight of the time."

"Is he a dish?" I asked.

"About fifty, thinning hair and suffers from B.O."

"My kind of man," I joked.

"I'm sure you could do better than him. Anyway, he's got a wife and three kids. He was telling me about his youngest, Amy

I think. That was what almost made me late. She's got herself in the club. Seems she and her boyfriend thought if they did it standing up, she wouldn't get pregnant."

I frowned. "She won't, will she?"

Mary looked at me with astonishment written all over her face. I couldn't hold my serious countenance any longer and began to grin at her.

"Bloody fool! It amazes me what they teach the kids at that comprehensive, it really does."

"Kids today." I croaked out in my grandfatherly voice.

"Absolutely!" Mary said, sweeping past me to change the date on the stamps that we used to indicate to the readers when their books were due back. That task accomplished, she announced, "Shall we open up then?"

"Yes, might as well let the madding crowds in." I went to the doors and unlocked them, swinging them back with a dramatic flourish. Of course there was no one waiting to gain admittance.

"Bloody fool!" she repeated. "You seem pretty happy today."

"Yeah, I'll tell you about it later," I replied. "Though I'm not sure you'll approve."

She raised an eyebrow. I could quite easily predict what her reactions would be. First would come shock. Then she'd wonder at my boldness. Next would come a short period of silence as she processed the information. Then she'd worry I'd put myself in danger. Finally she'd ask if I was going to repeat the experience.

Patrons trickled in throughout the morning. The miserable weather no doubt encouraged some people to just come in for a bit just to shelter from the rain.

We had the usual crop of students doing that last minute bit of research, needing to look up a few references for the essay that would be due in that day. We also saw a couple of local historians who wanted to consult the microfiche records of the local paper. Two old age pensioners shuffled through the doors.

The first wanted to find out what he could about a murder committed half a century ago. The second wanted to research his great uncle Frank, and whether or not he had won first prize for his onions in the county flower and produce show twenty-five years ago.

All pretty mundane stuff, but that was what I liked. Predict-ability, order and onions. The local historians knew what they were doing, so needed little help from me. The guy checking on the prize-winning onions wasn't really sure what to do, so re-quired more assistance. It seemed there was a long running fam-ily argument about whether Uncle Frank came in first or sec-ond. The things families argued about! I was able to find out he had actually got a 'highly commended.' No doubt this didn't satisfy either of the warring factions, but there it was in print, and so at least that particular argument was laid to rest.

The day progressed pretty much as most days do in the glit-tering world of non-fiction. As Mary and I took different lunches we couldn't talk then. I would have to wait till a lull in the rush.

It wasn't until half past three that the section was empty enough for me to feel I could spill the beans about the previous evening without being overheard.

"Want to know what I did last night?" I said to Mary as I sidled up to her left side, using my best master spy voice.

"I've been wondering what has improved your mood today, and the bit about me not approving has me intrigued."

"Well," I coughed, looked around again to ensure I wasn't going to be overheard and said rather too quickly, "I spent the evening with a male prostitute."

She laughed. I looked sternly at her.

"You didn't!" she said a bit too loudly.

"Not so loud! I did. Honestly."

She was stunned. I didn't think much would shut Mary up, but this did. She stared open mouthed at me for a few seconds. "Well, I'll go to the foot of our stairs."

Despite my nervousness, I had to smile at her old-fashioned turn of phrase.

"What was it like? You were safe weren't you? Did he hurt you? Will you do it again?"

I gave another quick look around. No one was paying us any attention. "To take each of your questions in turn, it was pretty nice. In fact I felt good about it."

Her eyes widened in surprise.

"Yes I was perfectly safe. We went to my place. All we did was sit on the sofa and kiss and cuddle. No, Mark—his name was Mark—didn't hurt me at all. I felt nice and warm and tingly inside." I closed my eyes to try to recapture some of the pleasant feelings of the previous evening, but I couldn't. I opened my eyes; the doubt was already beginning to settle in. "It's a pity I had to pay for the experience though." I sighed.

Mary gave me a hug.

"Thanks." I returned her hug. "Even though we agreed on a couple of hours he stayed later, and didn't want any extra money."

"That's, uh, good?"

I wanted to tell her more about Mark. Maybe talking about him would help recapture the good feelings. "I fed him. I don't think he'd had a decent meal in a couple of days. He was wearing a thin T-shirt on top, so I gave him an old jumper of mine. It was raining, so I also made him take an old raincoat. Honestly, Mary, I don't know where I got the courage to go out and do it, but I'm really glad I did." I paused, then said, "But I didn't give him my recipe for Yorkshire pudding."

She looked at me strangely for a few seconds. Then the penny must have dropped and she tilted her head back and laughed.

After she quieted, she asked, "Will you see him again?"

I shrugged. Part of me thought I'd pushed my luck the first time and it would be impossible to recapture the magic of that night. Another part of me thought I was weird and sad and creepy to be willing to pay for my happiness. And a third part thought *what the hell. Next time you can afford it, go for it!*

"I'm surprised, I really am. But if it makes you happy, then I suppose that's okay. Simon, you will be careful though, won't you? If you got hurt, I don't know what I'd do."

"I promise I'll be careful." Silently I added, *Careful with my heart, too.*

We continued with our duties until closing time. Bidding each other goodbye at the main door, we went our separate ways home.

I GOT BACK to the empty house, looked around and decided I'd have a bite to eat. I wasn't very hungry, so after heating up a few leftovers and eating them standing up in the kitchen, I went back into the living room and settled in front of the television news. I cuddled up with a big cushion. It wasn't a patch on snuggling up with Mark, but beggars can't be choosers, as my Gran would say—though I sincerely doubt she was talking about cushions and male prostitutes when she came up with that particular pearl of wisdom.

My mind drifted to thoughts of Gran. She's the closest relative I have. I love mum and dad, but I just don't have a close connection to them. But Gran—my mother's mother—is so in tune with me, it's scary at times. I remember coming out to her, trying to explain to the old dear how I felt about other men. The term gay didn't seem to explain things to her.

"Yes, love, I know you're happy," she'd said.

Eventually I'd just said, "Gran, I prefer to sleep with men. I honestly don't think I'd want to lie down with a woman."

"That doesn't mean anything," she'd said, waving a hand in dismissal. "I slept with your Auntie Flo for years: Auntie Flo was her sister; there were three brothers and two sisters in Gran's parents' three-bedroom house. Bless the old dear: she hadn't got a clue what I was talking about. As I'd stood there deciding whether to try and explain further, a twinkle had come into her eye. "Don't look at me like that. I know what a homosexual is. There was a talk on Woman's Hour on the wireless a couple of years ago about it. I was only pulling your leg. I don't mind who you love, so long as you truly love them."

"Aw, thanks, Gran, you're the best," I'd said as I gave her a squeeze and a kiss on her cheek.

My attention came back to the TV news: more killing in Northern Ireland. However, my mind soon drifted again.

I couldn't really remember my grandfather. He'd died when I was about five years old. He worked in a coalmine since he was a teenager, and the coal dust had gotten into his lungs. I had vague memories of a white haired old man coughing so hard I didn't think he'd ever be able to catch his breath. Mercifully he died quietly in his sleep, I think it was a heart attack, not directly related to his lungs. Gran didn't talk about him much, and I didn't like dredging up bad memories for her.

I never knew my grandparents on my father's side. A few years before I was born they died in a car accident while they were driving through Scotland.

The closing credits of the evening news brought me back to the present. Finding nothing else worth watching on the telly, I switched it off and put on a cassette.

I'd grown quite fond of classical music. I was able to borrow tapes from the 'audio-visual' section of the library, so I didn't have to lay out much expenditure on music. The hi-fi was a housewarming present from the folks back home. To the accompaniment of Beethoven's Pastoral Symphony, I got out a relatively recently published book on the moons of Jupiter that I'd borrowed from the library. I'd thought about getting a telescope, but a good one was out of my price range. Also, living in a town meant there was too much light at night to be able to see much. The book did say a good pair of binoculars was as effective as a reasonable telescope, and much cheaper. I'd have to give that some more thought.

I'd changed tapes a couple of times before my eyes began to droop, so I performed the usual nightly rituals before climbing the wooden hill to Bedfordshire, as Gran used to say to me when I spent the odd weekend at her house when I was little.

Chapter 3

THE NEXT COUPLE of weeks passed with mundane regularity. Putting out the dustbin on a Monday, doing several loads of washing on a Saturday. Things at work also carried on at their usual pace. The same faces, the same kinds of enquiries from readers thirsting for knowledge. All was comfortably plodding along in my little boring world. And also unchanging was my lack of a boyfriend.

I craved the physical comfort and security I could only gain from being close to another male. His smell, his warmth, the feel of his body close to mine. I needed all these and so much more.

After several typically uneventful days at the knowledge factory, I decided I needed a second Mark fix. I wasn't half as nervous this time as I headed towards Gamble Street. I just hoped he'd be there, and not with another customer. I really didn't want to imagine what he'd be doing with other people. I rounded the corner, and thankfully there he was. My heart lifted.

Jeez, I thought, *what's wrong with you? Surely I can't be developing feelings for this guy.*

I was able to damp down these feelings quite easily; I'd had plenty of practice. I played a game with myself, it was a self-defence mechanism. The percentages rule was what I called it. I'd read that approximately ten percent of the male population was gay. I wasn't too sure how they arrived at this figure, I just accepted it. The way my game worked was to remove those guys who were attached one way or another. Many gay men married women. Then there were those few lucky sods who managed to find a long-term boyfriend. Let's say attachments ruled out half of the gay population. These men were off limits to me. I absolutely could not be the 'other man'. I couldn't live with myself if I was the cause of a relationship breaking up. So by my calculations I was left with five percent. How many of these men were interested in forming a relationship? I had no idea of course. I surmised some men were content being alone. Then I guessed others preferred a long string of one-night stands. No commitment, no strings. The thought of this turned my stomach. I wanted—no needed—someone long term, permanent. Where did this leave the percentage tally? Let's say two percent.

It really doesn't matter if all the above figures were wildly inaccurate because the final determining factor was the killer. How many of these remaining men would be interested in someone as plain and uninteresting as me? I picture a decimal point with a frightening number of noughts, and just give up on the idea of ever finding someone.

Mark's welcoming smile had me instantly snapping out of my morose mathematical maundering. "Simon! Come for a return match, aye?"

I nodded, too embarrassed to speak. Mark gave me a quick hug.

Conversation on the way to my place was much easier this time. I knew he enjoyed movie musicals. We had also touched on the subject of books. Hey, I'm a librarian, what did you expect me to talk about? We both enjoyed biographies of famous people. All of this inconsequential chat lasted until we got to the house. As I shut and locked the door behind us, I asked if I could take his coat...my old coat. I was glad to see he was wearing it. It was now mid September, and the number of cold days was increasing. I'd been anticipating this moment ever since the last time I'd seen Mark, yet now it was here I grew shy. Mark seemed to understand. He sat on the sofa and patted the seat next to him. I smiled and complied with his unspoken request.

Quite quickly our arms were around each other again. I grew a little bolder.

"Can I kiss you?" I was able to ignore my incorrect grammar.

"I'd like that."

His head moved closer, and we engaged. The feelings that were running through my body were so difficult to describe. A warm, light-headed and all-over tingle.

After a short while I pulled back. "I went shopping the other day and should have a few goodies left. Have you eaten?" I asked, then winced at my stupid comment.

"Thanks, that would be nice," Mark replied, obviously choosing to go along with my odd behaviour.

We both got up together. I didn't want to break the body contact completely, so I held his hand and Mark didn't seem to mind. We went into the kitchen to see what was available. I suggested what British Rail would call an 'All Day Breakfast': bacon, sausage, mushrooms, tomatoes, and fried bread. I also scrambled a few eggs.

We decided to eat at the table in the kitchen. Our knees would often touch as we sat there and, when this happened, we would look up and smile at each other.

I loved watching Mark eat. He could really put away his food. I delighted in the fact I was able to help him in some small way. After all, he was helping me as well, by allowing me to hug and kiss him—although he wasn't shy about hugging and kissing me back.

After the meal was over, Mark offered to help with the cleaning up.

I refused. "You're my guest, and guests don't do the washing up."

Besides, I thought to myself, *I'll do it when you've gone, it'll take my mind off things.*

I'd lit the fire in the front room on our arrival, so a nice blaze greeted us when we retired to the sofa. We'd decided to listen to some music. Since I knew Mark liked classical, too, I offered to play the Beethoven Pastoral symphony that I'd still not returned. I was pleased to learn Mark was pretty knowledgeable about the piece.

"'An early example of programme music,'" he read from the liner notes.

I'd read the little booklet myself earlier, but I liked hearing Mark's soft, deep voice close by my ear.

"'The first movement—Pleasant Feelings on Arrival in the Country uses seven distinct motifs in sonata form…'"

I closed my eyes and tried to imagine myself in the countryside, with Mark. We were in a meadow, he holding me in his arms, both of us soaking up the sunshine. It was heaven.

When the final movement ended I opened my eyes and looked over at the mantle clock. With dismay I saw my time was up. In fact it had ended about ten minutes earlier. I hadn't heard Mark's watch alarm go off.

Perhaps he didn't set it. *Hmm,* I thought.

"Time's beaten us again," I said, little above a whisper.

He let out a long breath. "Yes."

I didn't want to make him feel uncomfortable. I knew his time was valuable to him. If he didn't work, he didn't get any money. "I hate that you have to go. But I know you need to."

He gave me a tight squeeze, then a long kiss on the lips.

We both got up and I led him to the door, all the time holding his hand. I didn't want to let go, but knew I had to. I gave him back his coat, hugged him again and told him to stay safe.

"I'll see you again soon," I told him, opening the door.

"Looking forward to it." He smiled and turned away.

I closed and locked the door, then went back to the sofa and collapsed on it.

"Oh, God, this is awful. I wish you could have stayed." The opening of Charles Dickens' *A Tale of Two Cities* came to mind: 'It was the best of times, it was the worst of times.'

I could still smell Mark's cologne on the cushions.

I stretched out on the couch feeling pretty sorry for myself. Then I gave myself a thorough talking to, got up and went into the kitchen and cleaned up. After this had been done, I felt drained, and so went upstairs to the bathroom and ran a warm bath. I always felt better after a good soak. I'd bought some relaxing bath oils, and I was certainly glad of their calming effects that night.

Thankfully sleep came easily, and I drifted off to thoughts of holding Mark in my arms.

LIFE CONTINUED ITS predictable pattern over the next few months. The weather gradually turned colder and wetter. The shops in the town got out their Christmas decorations, and the Council put up strings of coloured lights between the lampposts all down the main street. They had also coughed up for a large pine tree in the town square, and wrapped lights round it. Fortunately the local vandals didn't wreck the thing. Although I didn't much enjoy walking home in the dark, it was nice to see the Christmas lights, and also to look in the shop windows at all the festive displays. The children's section of the library had the only windows, which faced the high street, so it was up to the staff there to trim up the library's contribution to the town's outward show of festive cheer. The staff got the children to make decorations, and along with an aged—but still functional—carved nativity set, this comprised the display.

Of course the Scrooges at the Council had refused to find any money for decorations, so Mary and I put up some sprigs of artificial holly in Non-fiction. Mary's mother had donated some coloured paper streamers to add to the effect.

Mary and I stayed late one night to put up the streamers in our section. Mary had a better head for heights than I, so she agreed to ascend the stepladder, though I was told under pain of death not to let go of it.

"And don't you be looking up my skirt, Simon," she said from the top of the stepladder.

"Aw, go on, just a quick peek," I whined. "You're no fun anymore."

She laughed. "Don't start, you'll have me off this thing."

Mary and I had grown even closer. We'd agreed to go out every Friday night. Sometimes we'd have dinner at a pub, other times we'd watch a movie at the town's single screen cinema. Once we even went bowling, but I was totally hopeless at it, so we agreed—much to my relief—not to do that again.

Of course we kept up our usual friendly banter, laughing out loud frequently. People would look round at us to see what was funny and not unsurprisingly, this caused us to laugh even more. We played our usual game of man watching, Mary giving me a poke in the ribs if a bloke looked our way.

"See him, Simon, the one in the red sweater? No, don't be so obvious about it. He's looking this way. Perhaps this'll be your chance."

"No, he's probably envious of me for being with you." I replied, giving the man a quick glance. He certainly looked strong and broad and…

"Do you think so?" Mary touched her wavy auburn hair.

"Why not? If I liked women, I'd be jealous of anyone being with you."

"Daft sod." She punched me in the arm.

"It isn't daft at all. You're a lovely lady, and the man who manages to club you over the head and drag you back to his cave will be a very lucky guy."

"I'm not sure I want to live in a cave." She frowned. "Not one without central heating anyway."

"Now who's being daft?" I chuckled. "He just better treat you right, otherwise he'll have me to answer to." I said, flexing my puny arm and chest muscles. This caused another bout of laughter.

THE MANY SESSIONS of man watching did eventually pay off. He had wide shoulders, black hair, really deep green eyes, and a smile so warm it could melt an iceberg at a hundred paces. Yes, the man watching paid off big time…for Mary.

We'd gone to the cinema on one of our regular Friday nights out. As we exited, we decided to grab a bite to eat. Although I don't much go for fast food, the Golden Arches were nearby, we were both in need of immediate hunger relief, so we got ourselves burgers and fries and sat at a table in the middle of the restaurant. Our conversation about the film was intermittent. It was getting late and I was wilting visibly. I wasn't much of a fan of late nights. I'd just as soon be tucked up in bed with Humphrey, my teddy bear.

I asked Mary a question, but didn't get a reply. I looked up at her from the half eaten remains of my burger to see her gazing over my left shoulder. I turned round, not so easy in the fixed seat, to see a vision of male gorgeousness in an equal state of rapture, looking at Mary. I turned back to her, she was still frozen in place. I waved my hand in front of her face. She only partially came out of her trance, and looked at me.

"He's hot!"

"Yeah, I agree, and from the looks of him, he thinks the same about you. Why don't you go over there and talk to him?"

"I'm out with you." She said this with not much conviction.

"Don't be daft. Go over."

I never thought I'd see anyone float, not without the benefit of water that is, but Mary pretty damn well floated out of her seat and towards this vision of male perfection. I saw her take a seat next to him. His eyes followed her every movement, and when she got close enough he stood to allow her access into the booth. I wasn't close enough to hear what they were saying.

After convincing myself she was having a good time, I returned to my burger. I resisted the temptation to turn around and look at them, or should I say him? I dragged out eating the rest of the plastic meal for as long as I could, but the pressure on my bladder, and an ever-increasing need to get home to my bed, finally convinced me to get moving.

Before leaving, I approached their booth. "Mary, I'll be off now, I'll see you at work on Monday, okay?"

The vision spoke. "Oh, sorry, mate." Wow, what a deep warm voice. "I didn't mean to take your friend away from you."

"No problem." I waved away his apology. "Are you going to get the bus back, Mary?"

"Erm, yeah…erm Simon, I'll see you on Monday." She was obviously totally enraptured by him.

I couldn't blame her. I just gave a brief wave as I left. It was doubtful she even noticed.

After using the gents, I made my way out onto the street. Although it was December, it wasn't very cold. The wind, which had been pretty wild earlier, had dropped, so I decided to walk the fifteen minutes or so home.

MONDAY MORNING I unlocked and then relocked the door to

Non-Fiction after me. We had half an hour before letting in the public. The children's section opened at half past eight to allow the little darlings to change their books on the way to school.

Spotting Mary, I put my hand over my mouth, let out a high-pitched squeak, fell against the wall and said "My god, I'm in shock."

"Daft bugger," she replied. "I've been early before, you know."

"I can't remember the last time." And to be honest I couldn't. "Whatever could have caused this hitherto unforeseen event in the space-time continuum?" I'd just finished reading a science-fiction novel.

I was expecting a 'daft sod' or an eye roll. But instead I got a smile. I don't think I'd ever seen Mary smile so widely before. "He's called Jerry."

I didn't need to ask, but I thought I'd play dumb anyway. "Who is, the new milkman?"

"No, silly, the man we met at McDonald's."

"Oh!" I couldn't really find anything else to say.

Not surprisingly, Mary didn't have the same problem. The rest of the day—readers permitting—I got the full history of this god in human form. Apparently he was a post-graduate history student at York University. He lived in a flat with two other students close to campus during the week, and came home to visit his parents most weekends.

When Mary finally wound down, I asked, "So, he's the one then?"

The smile went up a few watts, and she nodded. Then her face fell a little.

"What? Is he married or something?"

"No, no, nothing like that." She shook her head. "Because he's away all week, I can only get to see him at weekends."

I was ahead of her. I'd worked it out earlier when she told me what his living arrangements were. "It's okay. You need to be with him as much as you can, I understand. We'll put our

Friday nights on hold for a bit." If the relationship was going where she hoped it was, we wouldn't be having any more Friday nights out for a long time, if at all.

"You don't mind?"

"Silly girl, of course I don't mind." I did, but I'd rather die than have her know this.

Mary was my only social contact—save for my occasional meetings with Mark—but she had as much right to happiness as anyone else. I'd really enjoyed getting out and about with someone for a change, but…putting my own feelings aside I could see Mary liked this guy a lot, and she needed time with him.

"You're such a sweetie," she said, kissing me on the cheek.

"Just don't forget to invite me to the wedding, you hear?"

"I won't."

I was half expecting her to make a joke of my last comment. The fact she didn't probably meant she was serious about Jerry. Most of me hoped it would work out for them.

Anyway, as I said earlier, the town was gearing up for Christmas. I'd bought the few presents I needed to. I posted off the ones to my parents in Birmingham. They'd moved down there a few years ago because Dad got a promotion, and after I'd finished university in Leeds I applied for and got the job at the library, so I stayed in the home town.

I had muddled along since my second meeting with Mark. I would take a walk down to Gamble Street once every couple of weeks or so. Usually he was there. If he wasn't, I'd carry on home and try again the next day.

Our times together—I wanted to call them dates, but was strangely reluctant to do so—followed the same path each time. I'd feed him, we'd touch and kiss for a bit, then we'd go into the living room and cuddle for a while on the couch. When the time came for him to leave, he would offer to stay later. I would tell him I really wanted him to stay, yet knew he had to get going, and he would thank me for being so understanding.

During our times together Mark had begun opening up to

me. He told me a little about his family background. It seemed his father was a brute. Things had been tolerable while his mother was living, but when she'd died of breast cancer, his father had hit the bottle...hard.

Up until this point I hadn't even been sure if Mark was gay. I realised he wasn't selling himself by choice, but some men have so few options that, despite being straight, they had to sell their bodies for sex in order to survive.

I suspected Mark hadn't told me the whole story about his family situation. It had been enough to start the waterworks in both of us though. I clung on so tight to him that evening, offering him what little comfort I could.

Another time he told me something about how he got into the business of selling himself. It wasn't a pretty story. He did say he was able to crash at—for want of a better word—his pimp's house. I grew so angry at the news of how Jake, the pimp, took half Mark's money in exchange for keeping Mark *safe* on the streets.

"Couldn't you just give him a bit less, and keep more for yourself?" I'd asked.

"No; John, another of Jake's boys, tried that. He was in hospital for over a month..."

I really wanted to get Mark out of his situation. I offered to help him. But it seemed as though Jake had a pretty tight rein on things, and I, too, could end up being hurt. I didn't see what I could do: I'm not—to my shame—very brave.

Chapter 4

IT WAS THE week before Christmas. I'd been walking along Gamble Street for the past three days, with no sign of Mark. I had mixed emotions about this. The weather was really cold now, so I was glad he wasn't out in the harsh weather so much, but I was missing him. I had grown very fond of him; I could quite easily be falling in love with him. Of course I couldn't tell him this. It was unlikely he'd feel the same way about me, and if he rejected me, even though he'd probably do it as gently as it could be done, I'd be devastated. I'm not very good at handling rejection.

By the fourth day of not seeing Mark I was beginning to get worried. Knowing I needed some answers, I timidly approached one of the other boys I'd seen on the corner near Mark before.

"Um, have you seen Mark? I've walked down here for the past few days, but he's not been around and…"

The guy looked at me for a moment. He seemed to come to a decision and asked, "You Simon?"

"Yes."

"Mark talks about you sometimes. You've been good to him. We don't get many johns who care about us, but you've made a real impression on him."

"Err, thanks. I do really care about him. I'm getting worried because I haven't seen him for a while. It's not like him."

"He's in hospital. Got burnt."

A bolt of electricity shot through me. My mind went frantic, a thousand images flashing through my mind. *What happened to my beautiful Mark?* "Was it Jake, did he hurt him?" I remembered Mark's comments about the guy who tried to cheat on Jake, and what happened to him.

"Not exactly. Mark probably told you he was staying with Jake. Well him, Jake I mean, and a couple of his sidekicks decided to go into the drugs making business. They got some chemicals and other shit together and tried to mix 'em. The dumb fucks didn't know what they were doing and there was an explosion. Jake was killed. No great loss there."

I couldn't disagree with him on that point, but I needed to know how Mark was. Was he badly burned? Would he live? So many questions came to my lips, but I just couldn't speak. I was frozen with fear.

The guy continued. "Both Jake's cronies were really badly burnt up. Mark was a lot more lucky though. I don't rightly know what's wrong with 'im, but I think he'll be all right."

"Is he in The General?" I managed to find sufficient breath to ask.

"Yeah, Bobbie, one of his mates, visited him the other day."

"Which ward?" I had to get to Mark.

"Um, dunno. Hang on a sec." The man yelled over to one of his colleagues, who yelled back "Ward Four!"

I turned and ran back to the high street, completely forgetting to thank the guy for the news. Hopefully he'd understand. I needed to get a bus to the hospital as soon as I could.

It's odd, I've always been pretty lucky about buses. Even when the service is really sporadic, I generally never have to wait longer than five minutes for a bus. I prayed damned hard my luck would hold today. It did. The number 14 turned up just a couple of minutes after I reached the bus stop. Of course—it being rush hour, and near Christmas—the bus was packed and I had to stand. I didn't mind. I don't think I could have sat still anyway. With agonising slowness the bus wound its way through the streets. Honestly, I don't think I've ever spent a longer ten minutes in the whole of my life. Every time the bus stopped to drop off or to pick up passengers, I raged inwardly at how long it was taking to get to Mark. I could barely contain my anger at the seemingly inconsequential lives I perceived my fellow passengers were living. Women heavily laden with presents for their undeserving brats back at home. Young men staring with vacant expressions out of the bus window, lazily chewing gum while their girlfriends applied more make-up to their already overly made up faces.

Pull yourself together, Simon. You'll be no use to him if you get yourself all worked up.

I managed to perform a few deep-breathing exercises, which helped me to calm down somewhat.

After what seemed like an age, the bus finally pulled up at the hospital gates. I almost wrestled an old lady to the ground in my haste to get off the bus.

I knew where ward 4 was. I didn't need to consult the hospital's useless signs. The moron who designed them had the worst sense of direction I'd ever come across.

I'd volunteered a couple of years ago to take the library trolley around the wards. It was a bit of a busman's holiday to swap one library trolley for another, but that was me.

I got to the entrance to Mark's ward completely out of

breath. I stood outside for a couple of moments to compose myself. Having regained my equilibrium, and with some trepidation, I pushed open the door and entered.

It didn't take me long to find Mark. My angel was asleep.

I knew from personal experience you had to grab your shut-eye when you could in a hospital. I'd had to spend a week in one just after leaving school. The nursing staff would wake me up in the evening to give me a sleeping tablet. Then at six o'clock in the morning they'd wake me up, because 'patients had to get all spick and span for breakfast'. God, the food was awful. I'd have preferred to sleep through it.

I quietly pulled a chair next to Mark's bed, although not before taking a peek at his chart. I was able to learn Mark's hands—which I could see were bandaged—had received moderate chemical burns. The doctors predicted a full recovery apart from the possibility of slight scarring. Mark had a few minor cuts and bruises, but nothing too severe. The chart said he was twenty years of age. I'd never actually got around to asking him how old he was.

The relief I felt that he'd live, that he'd be okay, overwhelmed me. For the past half hour or so I'd been gripped by a fear I might lose him, or he'd be badly scarred, or…I didn't care even if he was scarred. I loved him. I finally admitted the fact to myself I loved the beautiful, kind, gentle man lying in that hospital bed. I began to cry.

"Hey, it's me who ought to be crying."

Mark's soft, croaky voice brought me back from my thoughts. "Hey, Mark," I said. Wow, what a bloody inane thing to say. "How are you? Are you in much pain?"

"These hurt sometimes," he said, holding up his hands. "But they give me pills which take away the pain for a while."

"How long have you been in here? I wished you'd called me, or asked one of the nurses to."

"Just over a week. I thought about you, but…I didn't want to be a burden."

"Mark, you're never a burden. I found out from a guy on Gamble Street—I think he's a friend of yours: dark hair, kind of bushy eyebrows, pierced left ear with a gold hoop in it—"

"Sounds like Sammo."

"Okay, well, until I spoke to Sammo I had no idea you'd been hurt. Sammo didn't know how bad you were. So I got here as fast as my legs and the number 14 could carry me."

He gave a weak smile.

"Sammo told me there was an explosion. Something to do with Jake trying to make drugs or something."

"Yeah, he'd got some stupid idea about making more money, but I guess he didn't know what he was doing. I was in the room next door when I heard a really loud bang. I went in to see what I could do. It was horrible. They were screaming and carrying on. I got some of the stuff on my hands, and it bloody hurt."

"You know Jake died, don't you?"

"Yeah, one of the policemen who interviewed me told me. Can't say I'm sorry. Jake was an evil bastard."

I'd never heard Mark swear before, but I couldn't help agreeing with him.

"When are they letting you out?"

"I don't know. They'll have to find somewhere for me to go. Can't go back to Jake's. The Council has boarded it up, and with these hands…" He looked down at his bandages.

I had a decision to make. I could help Mark. I could look after him, nurse him, and—God help me—love him. I thought it unlikely Mark could love me back, but as I sat there I became absolutely certain I had a duty to help him. Given what Mark had told Sammo, I thought Mark at least liked me as a friend. Certainly his behaviour towards me was that of a friend. So with a determination—the likes of which I hadn't felt in years—I stood up.

"Have to go to the lav, back in a minute."

I didn't need to use the toilet, but I was on a mission, a

mission to help Mark. I left the bay where Mark's bed was, turned the corner and went towards the ward sister's office. Finding the door partially open, I knocked.

"Come in," a female voice answered.

I pushed the door open to reveal a forty-something, plump woman wearing a dark blue uniform dress sitting behind a desk.

"Sister, sorry to bother you. Have you got a minute?"

She smiled tiredly. I could tell she was over-worked. "Of course. How can I help?"

"It's about Mark Smith in bed eleven." I took the seat she pointed to.

"Yes?"

"I'm assuming the only reason he's still with you is that he has nowhere else to go, and given the fact that he can't use his hands, you can't discharge him until you've found somewhere for him."

"Are you a relative?"

I shook my head. "I'm a friend. Mark's mother is dead, he's estranged from his father, and he has no brothers or sisters."

I actually didn't know if Mark had any siblings, but I didn't think telling such a lie—if lie it was—would hurt. Besides, any brother or sister who could stand back and not help Mark when his father did what he did, wasn't worth much.

"You are correct, Mister…" She hesitated, not knowing my name.

"Peters, Simon Peters."

"Mr Peters. It's true Mr Smith doesn't need medical care as such."

I nodded. "I only just found out he'd been hurt. I lo…I mean I'm sure I'll be able to cope. So long as he gets a professional to change his dressings."

She smiled; she knew what I'd almost said. "Mr Smith can't do very much for himself."

"Yes, Sister, I know I'll have to feed him, bathe him, even attend him while he uses the toilet." This was a polite way of saying I'd have to wipe his bum. I'd do that in a heartbeat. "I guess it's a bit like looking after a baby; you have to do everything for them."

"It's similar," she smiled again, "although you'll have to cope with his mood swings if he develops them. Patients who can't do things for themselves tend to get very frustrated."

I nodded. "I'm sure I can cope. Besides, it's almost Christmas, and I'd hate to think of him stuck in here when he could be at home with me."

Her smile widened. "Have you discussed this with Mr Smith?"

I shook my head. "I wanted to see how the land lay first. I guess I didn't want to promise something I couldn't deliver."

"Thank you for being so understanding. It's true, we do try to discharge as many patients as possible at Christmas time. It's better for them, and of course we are short staffed over the holidays. Go back and talk to him, and if he's agreeable, I'll ring the doctor on-call and arrange for Mr Smith's discharge."

I shot out of that office as though there was a herd of wild animals in hot pursuit.

"Don't run!" she called after me.

But I was still on my mission to spring Mark. All I had to do now was convince him he had to come with me.

"Whoa, what's the hurry? Mark said.

"Mark," I paused to catch my breath, "I absolutely will not take no for an answer. I've thought it over carefully, spoken with the medical staff, and I am totally serious about this."

He looked confused.

"I want you to come home and live with me." I held up my hand to stop his protest. "You're not going to spend Christmas in this place. You're going to stop with me for as long as you want." I hoped he would want to stay for a long time, but kept that to myself.

"Urm."

"I can take some time off work, and there's The Holidays as well. And if you still need to be cared for, you can come to the library with me sometimes." I got very close to his ear and said quietly "I don't want you to go back onto the streets, it isn't safe. I'd not be able to rest knowing you were in danger. You've been given another chance now Jake is dead. Please, please, Mark."

He didn't say anything for the longest time. I grew more and more convinced he would refuse.

"You've thought all this out, haven't you?"

Was Mark going to do it? I nodded, but said nothing, holding my breath, hoping…praying.

"You know I can't do much for myself."

I nodded. "Yes, I've thought it through, and I know you'll need a lot of help."

He went quiet again. Maybe a minute passed before he sighed. "Okay, you win."

"YES!" I exclaimed a bit too loudly. A few of the other patients and their visitors looked at me, but I didn't care.

Eventually, after a load of form filling, and a letter to be given to Mark's family doctor explaining his injuries and treatment, and to make arrangements for his dressings to be changed by the nurse at the doctor's surgery, we were on our way.

At The General, as with many other hospitals I suspect, patients have to be escorted from the hospital in a wheelchair. It doesn't matter what's wrong with you, in Mark's case he had injured his hands. He could walk, but no, he had to sit in a wheelchair. The nurse pushed Mark in the chair as far as the hospital's main foyer, where we could ring for a taxi.

One good feature in the foyer was a direct and free phone to one of the local taxi companies. All you had to do was pick up the receiver and press the button. The only trouble was rival taxi companies didn't like this arrangement and frequently vandalised the phone. Of course sods law was in evidence here, the phone didn't work. The kind nurse who escorted us down went to the reception desk and got the receptionist to call a cab for us. This done, she departed with the wheelchair back to the ward.

"Shouldn't be too long," I said to Mark.

"Good, I'm getting hungry."

"Yeah, the food is pretty crap in here isn't it?"

"Bloody well is," he said with feeling. "The most edible thing we had for lunch today was the skin off the rice pudding."

I pulled a face. "Never mind, I've got plenty of food in at home. Stocked up for Christmas as usual."

"Thanks," he said quietly.

What is it about the British? We go around like headless chickens for a few weeks before Christmas, buying in tonnes of food. Much of the non-perishable items are still in the larder come April.

The taxi ride home was uneventful, the rush hour having long since passed, so it only took a few minutes to get us home. I paid the fare and got us inside.

As soon as the door closed behind us, Mark wrapped his arms around me and gave me a tight squeeze. "I don't know what I'd have done if you hadn't come along. I was beginning to think I'd have to go back home to Dad." He gave a shudder.

"You're stopping here." Tears began to threaten. "I get lonely stuck in here on my own. I want you to stay. Now you've got a permanent address." I hope he understood what I meant by permanent. "You can apply for state benefits, and hopefully when your hands heal, you'll be able to get a job. That should also be easier now you've got a proper home."

He kissed me.

"Come on, you said you were hungry. Let's raid the kitchen." I put my arm around his shoulders and led him into the other room. I opened the main cupboard door and said, "So, what do you want?"

"Erm." He stared into the cupboard, then, looking back at me, asked, "You remember the first time I came here and we had chicken and pasta?"

I nodded.

"Can we have that again?" He lowered both his voice and

his head. "It's kind of symbolic, I suppose."

"Of course we can." I swallowed. I was beginning to get emotional again. "You sit down there on that stool and remind me what we did last time."

I had to turn away from him to hide my eyes, which were starting to leak.

He directed operations while I prepared the meal. Thinking back to a psychology book I had once read, I realised it was a good idea to get him involved as much as his disability would allow. It would lessen the chances of him feeling helpless.

I put the two plates of food on the kitchen table and asked him if he wanted anything to drink.

"Water, please."

I filled two glasses from the tap. Then I rummaged around in the cupboard and found a packet of drinking straws. Putting a couple in Mark's glass, I took the drinks to the table.

"At least you'll be able to take a drink on your own," I said. More psychology.

"Thanks."

I sat at 90 degrees from him. Picking up my fork, I stabbed a bit of food with it and raised it up to Mark's lips.

"Open wide for the choo-choo train," I said with a smile.

He laughed.

While he was chewing, I put a forkful in my own mouth. We continued to eat. Mark bent down occasionally to take a sip of water. All in all I think we managed pretty well.

"I think in future, I may as well put both portions on the same plate," I said, bringing a piece of paper towel to his mouth to wipe up the spills. "It's odd isn't it? I can see where I'm putting the food when I feed you, but I make more of a mess than when I'm putting food in my own mouth, which I can't see."

"Yeah, but then you're used to feeding yourself. Probably just a matter of co-ordination and muscle memory."

"Yeah, probably." I replied. "Have you had enough? I think there might be some ice-cream in the freezer."

"No, I'm full, thanks," he said as he broke wind. "Sorry." He flushed red.

I smiled. "In some countries it's regarded as a compliment, and anyway, being laid down in bed does cause you to suffer from trapped wind. If you feel a bit bloated later, let me know. I've got some pills you can chew that should help."

"Thanks. Talking of pills, could you get me out a couple of pain killers that the hospital sent?"

"Your hands hurting?" I asked.

He nodded.

I found the pills and popped them in his mouth. He bent down and took a sip of water.

"Do you want to stay in here and talk while I clean up? Or would you like to go and watch a bit of telly?"

"I saw enough of the idiot box on the ward. I never was much of a telly addict."

"Me neither," I confessed. I used to spend most of my time at home listening to music, usually while reading a book or a magazine.

Mark remained where he was at the table, and I cleaned up. That done, we both went into the living room and sat on the sofa. I'd forgotten to light the fire. The central heating was on so the house wasn't cold, but things were always more cosy when the fire was lit.

I looked over at the mantle clock. It was a little after nine. "There's not much point in lighting the fire this late."

"No, I agree." Mark put his arm around me.

"Feeling okay?" I asked.

"Very." He yawned.

"Are the pills making you tired?"

He yawned again. "Yeah. It was difficult to sleep on the ward."

"I know. Do you want to take a bath or something?"

"I think I'd better, I don't know how much longer I'll be able to stay awake."

We headed upstairs into the bedroom.

"Back in a minute, I'll start running the bath."

"Thanks."

On my return, I said, "Right then, we better get these things off you."

"You remember the doctor said to put plastic bags on my hands and tie them shut with tape?"

"Oh, yeah, sorry." I ran downstairs, got a couple of large freezer bags and some bandage tape and began to climb the stairs again. I first went into the bathroom and turned off the bath taps, then back into the bedroom.

"Okie-dokie, I've got the stuff."

I found Mark sitting on the bed, hugging my teddy. "I see you two have made friends."

"What's his name?"

"Humphrey."

"Aw, that's a good name."

"We've been together a while now," I said, smiling at the pair of them. "The bath is ready if you are."

Mark put Humphrey aside.

As I undressed Mark, I saw the bruising which had been mentioned on his chart. "How come you got these bruises, I thought you weren't in the room when the explosion happened?"

He fell silent for a time. "A couple of my customers got a bit nasty when I wouldn't do stuff I didn't like doing."

I put my arms around him and gave him a gentle squeeze. Then I cupped his face. Looking into his eyes, I said, "That's all over with now. No one, and I mean no one, will ever hurt you again if I have anything to do with it." I kissed him on the lips.

He returned the hug. "Thanks, Simon. You don't know what that means to me."

It was certainly interesting bathing Mark. I'd never been so intimate with another adult male before. I had no small difficulty in trying not to get an erection. Mark's penis was just perfect. Resolutely turning my attention away from between his legs, I focussed on his chest instead. That didn't help all that much. Although not overly developed, Mark's chest was broad, smooth and...

"I've got some witch hazel in the cabinet. It'll help heal these bruises."

"Thanks, they do get a bit sore sometimes."

Back in the bedroom after drying Mark, I asked, "What do you normally wear to bed?"

"Underpants normally."

I got out a pair that was in a small package that had come home with him from the hospital.

"Are these the only clothes you own?"

"Yeah." He looked at the floor. "Sorry."

"Nothing to be sorry about. We'll go shopping in the next couple of days and get you some more stuff."

Mark started to say something, but I put up my hand to stop him.

"I'm paying. One day, when you've started earning, and you've built up a bit of capital, you can pay me back if you must, but I promise I'm not in any hurry."

"You're a good man, I don't know what I did to deserve your help, but I'm so glad you're here."

"I'm glad to be able to help." I gave him a hug.

He sat on the bed and I put the underpants on him.

"Now get into bed. I'm going to take a bath myself, and then I'll be back in. Is there anything you need in the meantime?"

"No thanks, but if you could bring in another glass of water and a straw when you've had your bath? I might need a drink in the night."

"No problem."

I pulled the quilt up to his chin then kissed his forehead. "Back soon."

I don't know why, but I seem to do most of my thinking while lying in the bath. A bit like Archimedes, I guess. Though I make no claims to be as intelligent as he was. I allowed the hot water to soothe me as I reviewed the day's events, and what a day it had been. First I'd had the worry about not seeing Mark for a few days, then I'd been told he'd been hurt, but hadn't known the details. Then I'd found him, and the relief that he would get well again had been tremendous. I'd learned he would need a lot of TLC, which I was determined to provide. Then I thought about washing him here in this bath.

Oh, God, he's so perfect.

I couldn't believe how lucky I was that I'd been given the chance to care for him in such a personal way, and I'd be able to do so for the next few weeks, too.

Lathering up the sponge, I washed my arms.

I desperately hoped the close relationship with Mark wouldn't end when he got well again. I was pretty sure he wouldn't go back on the streets. From what little he'd told me, it wasn't pleasant. I hoped once he found a job, he wouldn't want to move out. How would I persuade him to stay? I was certain I couldn't tell him of my feelings. As Mark hadn't said how he felt about me…romantically, he might feel trapped, or obligated to love me if I said anything. That would be horrible.

I scrubbed at my thin chest, then rinsed.

I wanted, no, needed his love, but it would have to come from his heart, not out of a sense of obligation. No, I couldn't tell him how I felt. But by God I could and would show him! Actions speak louder than words.

I'd have to be careful to give Mark his space, not smother him. I would be there for him, to help him, to support him. I would demonstrate my love for him in any way I could. This—I realised—was probably the best chance I'd ever get in life to be loved. Mark wouldn't just be judging my book by its cover. Hopefully he was seeing the kind of person I really was inside.

I got out of the bath and dried myself, then brushed my teeth. I'd forgotten to brush Mark's. I'd tell him when I got into the bedroom. I'd worried at the hospital that I only had the one bedroom. I didn't confess this to the staff, but Mark and I had been left alone for a few moments during the discharge process, and I'd asked Mark if he would object to sharing a bed with me. I'd said it wouldn't bother me, but if he felt more comfortable, I'd go out and get a camp bed, and we'd take turns using it.

He'd told me I worried too much. "Of course I don't mind sharing. It'd be nice to sleep in a bed with someone who really cared about me."

So that little problem had been solved.

I walked out of the bathroom and, remembering Mark's request for water, went downstairs. Coming back upstairs, I went into the bedroom to remind him about brushing his teeth. Fortunately I'd recently bought a new toothbrush that was still in its package. However, when I entered the bedroom I saw he'd already fallen asleep. He looked so peaceful, lying there on his left side. All the horrors which he must have faced recently were forgotten for a brief time. No, I wouldn't wake him. He needed his rest.

I got into bed behind him and spooned up against him. I put my right arm between his chest and his right arm. I'd never been fortunate enough before to sleep with another man. I hadn't expected I'd ever be given such a privilege. I wondered if I'd be too keyed up to sleep. But I needn't have worried. I soon drifted off into the best night's sleep I'd had in ages.

Chapter 5

SATURDAY MORNING DAWNED bright, but cold. We both got out of bed and started our morning routines.

"Do you need the toilet?" I asked.

"Yeah," he grinned. "I need to do a number two."

I laughed.

"Okay then, to the bathroom with you."

When we got there, I pulled down Mark's underpants. I tried not to look at what was revealed, but couldn't help myself. Mark sat.

"Do you want me to leave the room while you do your business? I know some guys are shy about stuff like this."

"No, it's okay, it's just a bit embarrassing."

"Sorry." I touched his shoulder. "Try not to let it bother

you. I know it's odd, but it'll be okay."

After Mark had moved his bowels, I asked him to lean foreword a bit so I could gain access to his rear, and do the necessary cleaning up.

"You know this isn't the first bum I've had to wipe."

"Oh?"

"I was in hospital a few years ago with a burst appendix. They didn't have any beds free in the main ward, so I had to stay in the children's ward. There was a cute little five-year-old boy in for a busted elbow or something. His parents hadn't taught him what to do after using the toilet, so he would shout, 'I'VE DONE! I'VE DONE!' from the cubicle. Nine times out of ten there wasn't a nurse within hearing range, so muggins here, who had the bed nearest the bathroom, had to go in and wipe it for him."

Mark smiled. I asked him to stand and I pulled up his underpants.

"And besides, your bum is a lot cuter than his." I patted said bum.

Mark laughed, which pleased me. I'd managed to make light of what could have been a potentially awkward situation.

After I'd washed Mark and brushed his teeth, he sat back on the closed lid of the toilet while I did the same for myself.

I WAS GLAD to hear that Mark was hungry, so I decided to cook a full English breakfast. I poured some fresh orange juice into a glass with the now customary straws and put a large plateful of fried food on the table between us. We used the same feeding routine as the previous evening, and although eating took longer than if Mark could have fed himself, we did okay.

We had a fair bit to do that morning, so I got ourselves ready to go out. Mark said he'd better use the toilet again before we left, so we trooped upstairs to take care of it. I didn't think

I'd ever get tired of handling his equipment.

After that task was accomplished I made Mark sit on the closed toilet lid while I brushed his hair. Mark's black hair was fine, soft, and naturally curly. I took a little longer than was strictly necessary. I don't think Mark minded.

Once I'd finished I gave him a quick kiss on the forehead. "There, you're done."

"Thanks." He smiled up at me.

"To stop you feeling as though you're just tagging along, I'm going to make you wear my rucksack. You might as well be of use while I've got you." I grinned to let him know I was kidding.

He chuckled.

We descended the stairs. I put on our coats, got out the bag for Mark and fitted it on his back, making sure the straps weren't too tight.

After closing and locking the door, we walked towards the town centre. I explained what I thought was the best plan of attack.

"I'll need to go into the library and arrange some time off."

"Sorry I'm being such a burden."

I shook my head. "I've plenty of leave owing and I've got to use it up by the end of April, otherwise I'll lose it. I didn't take a holiday this summer so I think I've got almost three weeks saved up." I didn't tell Mark the reason I didn't take a holiday was because I hated having to go alone. "So if I take two weeks worth of leave, plus the bank holidays, you should be well on your way to being able to potter around the house by yourself by the time I'll have to go back. If you're not, I can always use the rest of the leave, or you could come into the library for half a day or so. I'm sure I'd be able to find you something to do."

"You're being very kind."

"Rubbish, it really is nice having someone around the place." I didn't add that I hated being alone at Christmas. I guess I could have gone down to Birmingham to see my parents, but they often worked through some of the holiday, and it really wasn't worth the hassle with the trains.

"After the library, I thought we'd go down to the DHSS and get some forms, so you could start getting unemployment benefit."

"Okay."

"Then I'm taking you clothes shopping." I could tell Mark was about to object, so I cut in, "Now, Mark, please, we've discussed this."

He looked at me and sighed. "I don't have much of a choice, do I? Doesn't mean I like it."

"It'll be okay." I gave him what I hoped was an encouraging smile.

ALTHOUGH THE LIBRARY opened Saturday mornings, I only had to cover alternate weekends. I'd just finished making all the arrangements in the main office regarding my leave request when Mary walked in.

"I'd have thought you'd have seen enough of this place without coming in on your half day off."

"Mary." I gave her a smile. "Something's cropped up and I'm taking some time off. You'll be on your own for the next couple of weeks. I'm sorry."

"Oh?"

"Yeah, this is Mark," I said, putting my hand on his shoulder.

"Please to meet you." Mark started to hold out his hand to shake, then must have realised he couldn't.

"Mark's hurt his hands. He's agreed to move in with me until they heal."

She raised her eyebrows slightly. She knew! "Oh, dear, how did you manage to do that?"

"Some people I knew decided to play around with chemicals, and things got out of control. Some of the stuff got on my skin."

"You poor thing. I hope this reprobate is taking good care of you," she said, pointing an accusing finger at me.

"He's been a godsend," Mark said, wrapping an arm around me.

I was so happy at his gesture, I couldn't get the silly grin off my face. Of course Mary spotted it.

"Shouldn't you be getting back to the department?" I asked her.

She stuck her tongue out at me as she passed us. Mark laughed, but I was used to her.

When she'd gone, Mark said, "She's a scream."

"Yeah, she is. She's got a heart of gold, though."

We left the library and walked to the government offices for the unemployment forms. Then we shopped till we dropped. I encouraged Mark to choose everything from a base-ball cap, which brought out the colour in his eyes, to a stout pair of shoes. He complained about how much it was costing.

"You need these clothes, so you're having them," I said with determination.

We stopped off at the surgery and got Mark registered with a doctor. Mark came from Newcastle originally; when his father kicked him out Mark simply bought a bus ticket to the furthest place he could afford. Although it was very selfish of me to think it, I was bloody glad he didn't have any more money than he had, otherwise our paths would never have crossed. Fortunately my doctor had some spare places on her list, so I was able to get him registered with her. She was a really kind lady who didn't judge. I knew Mark would be well looked after by her. We arranged for Mark to come in early the next week to have his bandages changed by the nurse.

So with everything done that could be done, we headed home.

"Phew, I'm glad that's done!" Mark said as he collapsed on the sofa after I'd taken the rucksack from him.

"Are you tired?" I asked with concern.

"No, not exactly. My hands are starting to hurt though. I don't know if it's because it was cold out there."

"Why didn't you say something? I took your pills with us."

I pulled the bottle from my pocket and showed him.

"Sorry, I didn't know you'd brought them."

"I'll get you some water, and you can take a couple now."

"Thanks.

"Do you want to lie down here for a bit while I get us a bite of lunch?" I asked Mark once he'd taken his tablets.

"Would you mind? These pills make me a bit sleepy sometimes."

"Of course not," I said, ruffling his hair. "I'll take off your shoes and you can get more comfy."

He gave me a kiss.

"Shall I light the fire?"

"That'd be smashing, thanks."

I hadn't set the fire that morning. I'd wanted to get on with the shopping. So I spent a few minutes cleaning out the grate and re-setting everything. Some people make setting the fire a real art form. I can honestly say I'm not that anal. So long as the newspaper, small sticks, and the coal are put on in the right order, I don't see the need to make a performance out of it.

The fire having taken hold, I went into the kitchen, washed my hands, and prepared a few sandwiches.

On my return to the living room, I spied Mark gazing into the flames.

"Penny for them."

This seemed to rouse Mark from his thoughts. "I love looking into a real fire. I imagine all kinds of shapes and stuff. It's hypnotic."

I smiled. "Some people say having an open fire is too much work. But I think it really makes a room look and feel cosy."

"Uh huh." Mark continued to stare into the fire.

I got out a TV dinner table and put the plate of sandwiches and snacks on it. Then I took Mark's glass, went back into the kitchen and refilled it, and got another glass for myself. Returning to the living room, I sat next to Mark and began to feed him.

After we'd finished eating, I lay across the back of the couch and Mark spooned back into me. I pushed one arm under him, and draped the other one over his chest.

"Happy?" I asked.

"Love being here…you holding me." He grew silent for a few minutes. I thought he'd dropped off, but he spoke again. "I used to stand on Gamble Street hoping that day would be the day I'd see you."

I kissed the top of his head.

"Sometimes it got pretty bad out there. One day I'll tell you more about it. I know I've told you a few things, but I'm not ready to talk about it yet."

I squeezed him and kissed the top of his head again.

"I felt safe, warm, and cared for when I was here. I always wanted to stay longer, but I knew I had to go and earn more money."

"You're staying now. I'm not letting you go." I hoped Mark didn't read the true meaning in my words. I'd have to be more careful in future.

Mark snuggled in closer and fell asleep.

We both jumped at the sound of the ringing phone. I extricated myself from Mark to answer it.

"Hello?"

"Hi, Simon."

"Hi, Mary. What can I do for you?"

"I wondered if you two wanted to go out this evening for a drink. As you know, Jerry is in the Middle East on his history field trip and I was at a bit of a loose end. I thought you might want to paint the town red."

"I'm not sure about red, it isn't really my colour."

"Daft sod!"

"Hang on, I'll ask Mark." I put my hand over the receiver and said, "Mary wondered if we'd like to go out for a drink tonight. I know it'd be a bit awkward to go out for a meal, but do you fancy an hour or two down the pub?"

"Yeah, it'd be nice to get out and relax for a bit." He paused. "I've no money though."

"That's okay, don't worry about it. Do you want to go?"

"Love to, thanks."

I raised the receiver to my ear. "We'll meet you at the White Swan, say about eight?"

"Great! I'll see you both there then. Love to Mark."

"Okay, bye-bye."

I replaced the phone back in its cradle and returned to the sofa. "Mary sends her love," I told Mark as I sat down and pulled him against me.

"Does she, erm, know about, I mean does she know how we met?"

I decided I'd always be honest with Mark, unless the information would unnecessarily cause him pain. I reached up and, cupping Mark's chin, turned his head to face me. Kissing him, I said, "Yes she knows what you used to do for a living. But as you've seen for yourself, she's a good person. I promise she's fine about it all. If you ever need to talk to someone, and you're not comfortable about telling me, then think about talking to Mary. Although she might look the gossipy type, she's the most loyal friend I've ever known."

He hugged me.

"Mary will make a play of trying to get the dirt on you, but it'll all be in fun. She wouldn't hurt anyone. She might get a bit protective over me, but it won't be long before she takes you under her wing, too."

"She sounds like a really good friend."

"The best," I said. "She's got a boyfriend, but he's on some kind of university field trip and won't be back until the New Year."

I chuckled as I related to Mark how Mary and Jerry met. Mark laughed at the comic scene I painted.

We spent the rest of the afternoon lounging about, listening to music, talking, and generally enjoying each other's company. About six we decided to make a start on dinner.

"Want anything in particular?"

He shrugged. "Whatever you feel like cooking is fine by me."

I looked in the kitchen cupboards, the fridge, and freezer. "How about a tin of chunky vegetable soup to start, then liver and onions? I want to build you up so you're nice and strong."

Mark gave me a hug. "Thanks, you're being really kind."

"You haven't had a very good diet recently. I just want to redress the balance," I deflected.

He gave me a kiss on the lips. It was wonderful. I tried not to read too much into the gesture, but it wasn't easy.

I sat Mark down on his now customary stool and got on with preparing our meal. Conversation was light and pleasant. I revelled in the cosy domesticity. I just hoped and prayed—not something I did often enough—that this, this whatever it was I had with Mark, would grow and strengthen with time. I got a bit worked up and a few stray tears began to fall. However, I was able to cover up my problem because I was slicing onions at the time.

Once we'd eaten, I asked Mark if he wanted a bath before we went out.

"Please, I wasn't able to bathe as much as I liked in hospital. They were short staffed, and I got embarrassed when the female nurses did it."

I laughed. "Weren't there any cute male nurses on the ward?"

"Just the one. But I was even more embarrassed the day he bathed me."

"Why? Your body is perfect." Now it was my turn to be embarrassed.

"Thanks., but…uh when the male nurse said he wanted to bath me I got an erection."

I laughed again. "What did you do, apart from turning red and getting hard?"

"I managed to delay him undressing me until it went down."

"Listen, Mark," I said, becoming serious. "If you ever need

me to relieve you, you know, I…would. I've never done it to another person before, so I don't know if I'd be any good, but I'd do my best to…" My embarrassment was returning full force, but I determinedly ploughed on. "I'd give you a hand." Then I realised what I said and felt my face get even hotter if that were possible.

Mark laughed. "Thanks." He too was going a little pink in the face. "I wasn't sure how I'd take care of that."

"Just let me know if it comes up." I scrunched my eyes closed. I'd done it again. "How come the floor never opens up and swallows you when you need it to?"

Mark laughed harder.

"I'll go and start running the bath," I said, making my escape.

Turning on the bath taps, I told myself that I'd have to be more careful in future about dropping hints like that. The last thing I wanted was for Mark to feel uncomfortable. However, I reasoned he would have needs and I couldn't imagine anything more frustrating than not being able to satisfy them. So I thought on balance I'd made the right decision about bringing up the subject. I'd allow Mark to say if or when he actually wanted me to help him out.

I waited until the bathwater had reached the desired height. I also decided I'd better check the temperature, so rolled up my sleeve and dipped my elbow into the water. I chuckled at the image that came into my mind. Mark walked into the bathroom at that point.

"What's so funny?"

"Did you ever watch the kids' TV show *Blue Peter*?"

"Yeah, why?"

"You remember whenever they bathed one of the pro-gramme's pet dogs, they always made such a play of testing the temperature of the water with an elbow. Something about that part of the body being more sensitive to heat."

"Oh, yeah, I remember now." He began to chuckle too.

I undressed him, put the bags on his hands, taped them up

and helped him into the tub. I knew I'd never tire of looking at his gorgeous—if slightly battered—body.

"I'll put more witch hazel on your bruises when we're done."

"Thanks, I didn't seem to hurt as much after the last lot."

"Good. Want me to wash your hair while you're in here?"

"Please."

I wet his hair and applied some of the apple-scented shampoo I'd been given for my last birthday. I got a bit turned on at the sensations I felt while running my fingers through Mark's curls.

"That smells nice," he said.

"I doubt it's ever been near a real apple," I said, "but it still smells nice."

"It's great."

"Right then, time to rinse off." I scooped up some of the bath water with a large beaker I kept for just that purpose, and repeated the hair washing as directed on the bottle. Normally I didn't bother re-applying the shampoo, as I'd read somewhere that it didn't actually clean the hair any further. It was just a way that the shampoo manufacturers got to shift twice the volume of product than was actually necessary. But I was enjoying the feeling of washing Marks hair too much to be prudent about wasting money.

Once I got Mark out of the bath, I pulled the plug and towelled him dry. He went into the bedroom while I ran another bath for myself.

Finished bathing, I put on a clean pair of underpants and went into the bedroom. I asked Mark what he wanted to wear to go out.

"Erm, I think I'd like to wear those 501's with a white T-shirt and that fluffy crew neck jumper you said looked good on me."

"It did."

"Yeah," he chuckled. "Okay, that's what I'll wear then."

Clothing choices made, I got to work dressing first Mark and then myself. I then had the pleasant duty of brushing

Mark's hair.

"You like doing that, don't you?" he asked with a smile.

I reddened. "Your curls are great."

Mark shrugged. "Genetics."

Hair brushed and coats on, we headed out.

We'd only just turned the corner out of our street when Mark stopped suddenly.

"What's wrong?" I asked in concern.

"No straws."

"They'll have some at the pub, but I probably should go back home, just in case."

"Thanks."

"Do you want to carry on walking, and I'll catch you up?"

Mark nodded.

I headed back to the house. It's amazing how many things you have to think about when you're caring for someone with a disability. However, I was more than pleased to be of whatever help I could to Mark. If his hands weren't bandaged he wouldn't be with me, and I'd...I didn't want to complete that train of thought.

On my way back to Mark, I heard raised voices. Getting closer, I could see it was Mr Simpkins, an oily little man who was trying to get into Marks face about something. From what I could pick up, it seemed Simpkins must have been one of Mark's previous clients, and he wanted Mark to perform for him again. Mark was doing his best to get out of Simpkins way, but with little success. I knew something of this obnoxious example of pond slime, so I inserted myself between them.

"Hello, Mr Simpkins. I saw your good lady wife last week. I hope she's enjoying that book I managed to get for her on Roman pottery."

The best description of Mrs Simpkins was "formidable." I had no problem with her at all. She'd been a regular at the library for years, and I often managed to source reference books on ceramics and pottery for her. She was something of a collector. She—and the henpecked Mr Simpkins—would scour the local car-boot sales to add to her impressive collection.

At seeing me, old Simpkins wilted considerably. I put a protective arm around Mark.

"I was just talking to this, this…"

"Yes, this is my very good friend, Jim." I remembered Mark's street name. "I'm sure Mrs S wouldn't be too pleased to know what you were about to ask Jim to do, would she?"

Simpkins went white. I began to feel a little sorry for the old man. He didn't have much freedom in his life. Mrs S certainly wore the trousers in their house.

Simpkins turned and fled the scene. I faced Mark, putting my other arm around him and giving him a tight hug. I don't think anyone saw us. I wasn't particularly bothered if they had.

"You were great," Mark said quietly. "I couldn't have handled him like that. He was one of my…shall we say…less pleasant clients."

"Don't worry, love. I've got his number. His wife keeps him pretty well under her thumb. I suppose he was just trying to get back some of his macho image, but he absolutely will not do it at your expense. I won't let him, or anyone else."

Mark gave me a squeeze. "I'm so lucky to be living with you."

"I'm the lucky one," I whispered.

He gave me a final squeeze, then disengaged from the hug.

"You ready to go on?" I asked. "Or would you rather go home?"

"I'm not going to let the likes of him spoil the rest of my life. I didn't enjoy what I had to do, but I had no option at the time."

"You've got options now. Come on, I think you need a stiff drink."

"Better stick to something soft 'cause of my pills."

"Yeah, sorry."

We completed the rest of our journey to the pub in silence, but I felt it was a comfortable rather than an uncomfortable one. In a town the size of ours, he was bound to encounter old clients. Most wouldn't acknowledge that they knew Mark, but the odd one like old man Simpkins wouldn't have the brain or the tact to stay away. I'd be there as much as I could to help Mark cope.

We arrived at the White Swan, or the Mucky Duck as it was known by the majority of its regular patrons. Of course Mary hadn't arrived yet. I don't think she'd ever arrived anywhere early. I hoped Jerry could come to terms with her timekeeping.

"What'll it be, gents?" Ron, the barman, asked.

"I'll have a pint of your best bitter, please," I replied. I looked at Mark for his choice.

"Tonic water, please."

"Coming right up."

"Oh, and could I have a dry Martini for our other guest, who hasn't shown up yet?"

"Sure. Waiting for Mary?" Ron asked.

"As ever!" I sighed dramatically.

Ron laughed.

Ron put the drinks on a tray, I paid and we went to sit at a table in the far corner. I sat facing the door so I could spot the latecomer when she arrived.

"It's nice in here," Mark said.

I nodded after taking a pull on my pint. "Mary and I used to drink here. Mind you, that was in the pre-Jerry days."

We made small talk until madam Mary showed up. When I spotted her, I winked at Mark. "I wonder what excuse she'll have this time."

"Is she often late?"

I grinned. "Almost always."

"Hello, boys."

"I got you one in," I said, pointing at her glass.

"Thanks, I need it."

"Oh?"

"Yeah, just come off the phone to Jerry. He seems to be

having a whale of a time out there. Says he misses me, though."

"Aw, ain't love grand," I put in.

"Yes it is. Speaking of which, how are you two love birds getting on?" Fortunately no one was sat close by, and Mary spoke softly.

I was expecting such a comment, but Mark wasn't. He reddened, but quickly recovered.

Mark put his arm around me and said, "We're getting along great, thanks."

This caused me to go red, and Mary to laugh.

"You've got a keeper there, Simon." She smiled.

I looked at Mark and said, "Yes, I think so too."

Mark just smiled. I began to wonder if he really did think something of me. I'd have to tread very carefully, but his smile certainly lifted my spirits.

"Tell me, Mark," Mary asked, "Have you picked up any good recipes for Yorkshire Pudding?"

Mark looked confused, and I kicked Mary under the table.

"Ouch!"

"I'm not with you," Mark said.

I glared at Mary then turned to Mark. "Never mind, I'll tell you later."

The three of us spent a very enjoyable evening in the pub. Although I was very much a homebody, I occasionally did enjoy a change of scene, especially when out with such convivial company.

"Well, boys, Dad will be picking me up out front in a couple of minutes, so I better not keep him waiting. I hope you'll be thinking of me sleeping all on my ownsome tonight."

Keeping my expression as neutral as I could, I asked, "You could always join us if you fancied a threesome."

Mary blushed. This was a rare occurrence, so I felt as though I'd scored a minor victory. It was usually me who would end up embarrassed.

"No thanks, I bet at least one of you snores."

"Who said anything about going to sleep?" Mark put in.

I put a hand over my mouth to stifle a laugh. My man was learning how to handle Mary. Good on him.

"I think I better go while my virtue is still intact." She smiled. "Look after yourselves, you hear!"

"We will!" we both said together.

This caused all three of us to chuckle.

We escorted Mary to the door, and waited till her dad came to pick her up. Then we made our own way home.

"DID YOU ENJOY yourself this evening?" I asked Mark as we lay in bed that night, me spooning behind him as usual.

"Yeah, Mary's a lot of fun."

"She certainly is. Feeling tired?"

Mark yawned his answer. "I've had a really fun day. Thanks for everything."

"You're welcome." I kissed the back of his neck. "I've had fun, too."

The room fell silent.

I was just drifting off when Mark said, "Simon?"

"Yeah?"

"What was all that about Yorkshire Pudding?"

I chuckled, then told Mark about the silly game Mary and I sometimes played.

He laughed.

Chapter 6

WE WERE SITTING at the kitchen table on Sunday morning. I had just cleaned away the breakfast things, pleased Mark's appetite was still good.

"Do you want to get a start on those benefit forms we picked up yesterday?" I asked. "I doubt if they'll be processed before Christmas, but the sooner we get it done, the sooner they can start paying you."

"Yeah, okay. Might as well get it over with."

I got out the forms. It was amazing what the government needed to know before they'd part with a penny of the taxpayer's money.

"It's a good job we went clothes shopping yesterday," I said.

"Why?"

"Because I just know they're going to ask for your inside leg measurement," I said with a straight face.

"You twit."

"Look, Mark, they want details of what you've been doing for the past few years. I know you had a job in a supermarket up in Newcastle, but how do we explain the last 6 months?"

Mark went quiet for a moment. I knew this kind of question would be on the form.

"We tell them I was homeless, it isn't exactly lying."

"That's true!"

I carried on filling in the form. I had to ask him for the answers to many of the questions. After all, I had only known him for a few months, and many of the questions weren't the sort of things that cropped up in general conversation. After we'd finished, of course Mark wasn't able to sign the forms, but there was a section which I could sign to say I had filled the forms in for him.

"We'll need to get you a sick note from the doctor, because obviously you can't work at the moment."

"We can ask the nurse about that tomorrow when I have my bandages changed."

"Good idea. Look, I don't know about you, but all this form filling has given me a bit of a headache. Do you want to go out to stretch your legs?"

"Yeah, I could do with a walk."

"Right, we'll call in at the Chinese take away on the way back if you want. They do a fantastic sweet and sour."

Mark's face lit up. "I love Chinese."

THERE WAS A small wood about five minutes from the house, so we decided to walk there. Once we'd reached the security of the tree line, Mark put his arm around me. I did the same to him. We continued walking deeper into the woods in a comfortable silence. The only sounds came from the twigs snapping under our shoes and the birds singing up in the trees.

We spotted a fallen tree trunk. Without either of us indicating to the other, we both walked towards it, still with an arm around each other. However, we had to disengage in order to sit. Once settled, Mark put his head on my shoulder and gave a contented sigh.

"Comfy?" I asked.

"It's so peaceful here. Seems a world away from all the horrible things that've happened over the past few months."

"I know." I rubbed his arm.

Mark stayed silent for quite some time. He swallowed, then said, "I'm not a bad person. I'm not evil, I don't go around molesting little kids or anything like that!"

I wondered where all this was coming from. Then I had an idea. "Did your father accuse you of being those things?"

Mark shuddered. "Yes, it was horrible. I never really got on with him, but when he found me and Danny messing about in my room, he just lost it completely. He hadn't got over mum's death, BUT THAT WAS NO EXCUSE!" Mark shouted.

I said as calmly as I could, "No, it was no excuse. Your dad needs to seek professional help for his anger, but you're out of all that now. You had to leave, and I understand why you had to work on the streets like you did. I've never judged you, and I never will." I pulled him tighter into my chest. "You are a precious and beautiful human being, who—like the rest of us—deserves to be happy." This certainly was not the time to tell him he was the key to my happiness.

"I never told you all the details of why I ended up selling myself, did I?"

"You said you had no money, nowhere to live, but Jake let you stay at his place, so long as you worked for him."

"That's only part of the story. When I got off the bus in town I sat on a bench in the bus station. I had no idea what to do. I must have sat there for hours just glad I'd gotten away from my dad, but I'd run away without thinking where I was actually running to." Mark let out a long breath.

I kept rubbing his arm, offering silent support.

"It was getting dark, and I was wondering where I could spend the night. Although it was July, it had turned cold. I had only a few minutes at home to pack a bag. I didn't even bring a coat. Jake found me on that bench. He took me to a cafe and bought me something to eat and drink. I didn't realise how hungry I was. He talked to me. He really seemed like a kind person." Mark let out a humourless bark of laughter. "Was I ever taken in by him! He said I could stop at his place that night, and we'd talk about finding me somewhere to live and work the next day.

"Well, to cut a long story short, Jake loaned me some money so I could get a room as a lodger, and said he would see about finding me work. I was walking down the street a couple of days later, I had the money Jake had given me in my pocket, and I was mugged. I've never been so scared in my life. I, I, I pissed my pants." Mark was openly crying by this point.

I hugged him, almost pulling him onto my lap. Stroking his hair, I whispered comforting noises to him, although inwardly I was seething. I bet it had been Jake's thugs who had mugged Mark.

"It's okay, you're safe now. It's over."

Mark sniffed and slowly gathered himself together. "Because I had no money, I had to leave the lodgings. It was at this point Jake reverted to type. He wanted his money back, and told me I'd have to earn it as 'one of his boys'. Of course I didn't know what he was talking about…I soon found out. It was like being in a spider's web. Once I was in the web, I couldn't work out a way to get myself out. I don't know, I suppose I could have left town and tried somewhere else, but by this point I'd lost all my self respect, and I imagined I'd be in pretty much the same boat wherever I went. So I stuck it out. At one point I thought I'd paid off my debt, but I didn't realise

Jake was charging me interest on the loan, and I had to pay for the room at his place, too.

"Then you came along. At first I thought you were another weirdo like Simpkins, but all you ever did for me was treat me like a decent human being."

"Which is exactly what you are." I kissed the top of his head.

"Because of being able to see you, I managed to stick it out. Things weren't all bad. Some of the other boys on the street were kind to me. A few of my customers were okay, too. I don't know, maybe I'm just weak. Maybe I could have got out of it all if I'd have tried harder, but I didn't know what to do. You offered to help me that once. That meant a lot. But I was afraid Jake would come after you, too. I couldn't have stood it if that happened. So when Jake died, that meant I was free, but I had these bandages, and couldn't do anything for myself. Then you came to the hospital. I hoped you'd be able to help me somehow. But I never thought you'd do as much as you have."

"You've helped me, too. After a day at the library, I'd lock my front door, and never see or speak to another soul until I unlocked it again the next day. Having you come to live with me, though I wish it wasn't because of your hands, has...well, I've gotten a lot out of it."

"I guess we'll just carry on muddling along, helping each other, then," Mark said.

I hoped we'd do much more than that, but it wasn't the time to go into it then.

"I don't know about you," I told Mark, "but I'm cold and hungry. Do you still want Chinese?"

"Please."

We walked back to the house via the take away. Mark seemed so much brighter after unburdening himself. Although I could just about use a pair of chopsticks, I thought it would be easier—if unauthentic—to use a fork to feed Mark.

"I've never understood why some people say they are hungry again half an hour after eating Chinese food," I said to Mark as we lounged on the sofa after stuffing our faces.

"Me neither, it seems to fill me up in just the same way as any other meal." Mark snuggled up to me. This was rapidly becoming our favourite position, and I wasn't about to complain. "You know," Mark continued, "Chinese take away reminds me of home. A good memory, though. We'd do our supermarket shopping on a Thursday night. This was when Mum was still alive. On the way home we'd pick up a take away. As we walked around the supermarket, I'd be thinking about what I would order. Now every time I visit a supermarket, I can't help thinking about Chop Suey or special fried rice."

We both laughed.

"Why don't we make it a tradition here? I've always done the supermarket shopping on a Thursday evening as well. It wouldn't take us too much out of our way to get Chinese on the way home."

"Could we? That would mean a lot."

"Then that's what we'll do." I kissed Mark on the top of his head. He wriggled contentedly in my arms.

Flicking through the four TV channels we had in those days—this was before cable and satellite came on stream—we decided there wasn't anything worth watching. Mark decided he'd like to watch a video.

"So, what would you like to see?" I asked him.

"Have you got *Carry On, Doctor*?"

"Yes. It's my favourite one of the series."

"Mine too. I know it isn't a quality film, but it makes me laugh," Mark said.

"When it comes down to it, that's all that matters."

"True," Mark replied.

We cuddled up and watched the film. It was good to see Mark laughing after the painful revelations he had disclosed earlier in the day.

As the tape was re-winding, someone knocked at the door. I wasn't expecting anyone, so I slipped on the security chain before opening it.

"Can we sing a few carols for yer, mister?"

Three little boys, and an older boy, possibly a brother of one or more of them, stood on my doorstep.

I smiled. "Okay then."

In most places the carol singers would sing first and then knock on the door. However, this being the north of England, no bunch of carol singers worth their salt would sing to an empty house, or to anyone who hadn't promised to pay them after they had sung. Mark came and stood next to me by the partially opened door. We listened to a couple of carols—like all children, including myself at that age—they only knew the first verse of any carol. However, that didn't matter. It was one of the things which marked the beginning of Christmas for me. That and the Salvation Army band playing in the town square.

When the carol singers finished, I gave them 20p. Mark and I then wished them a Merry Christmas. I turned round after locking the door to face Mark. He was smiling.

"Aw, wasn't that sweet?"

"Christmas is certainly coming now."

"Do you think we could get a tree? I don't mean a real one. Just a small artificial one, with some lights and stuff?"

"Why not? I've never bothered with one before, but it would make a nice symbol of our first Christmas." The first of many, I hoped.

Mark's whole face lit up.

"And I suppose you'll want miles of tinsel, baubles and flashing lights too?" I asked, a smile on my face.

"But of course!"

"We need to go out tomorrow to get your bandages changed, so we can get all the stuff then. I think Woolies was having a sale on decorations the last time I looked."

"Great. Can we have a fairy for the top, too?"

I rolled my eyes and shrugged. "Why not?"

Mark laughed excitedly. Which to my ears was a wonderful

sound. I'd buy the whole of Woolworth's Christmas department if it would make him happy.

Just then the phone rang.

"We are popular this evening." I said as I walked towards the instrument. "Hello?"

"Hello, Simon." It was my mother. We rang each other on alternate Sundays as it was cheap rate at the weekend. We were Yorkshire folk, so of course we were careful with our money.

"Hello, Mum, how are you and Dad?"

"We're fine, love. I was just ringing to ask if you were coming down here for Christmas."

"Err, no, I've got someone staying with me this year."

"Oh?"

"Yeah, he would have been on his own, so I invited him to stay."

"That's nice. What's his name? Where did you meet him?"

My mother knew I was gay. Both Mum and Dad had accepted my coming out. However, accepted was about the best that could be said. I guess it was something to do with the ending of their dreams of having grandchildren. I was an only child.

"He's called Mark. We've known each other for a while now."

I wasn't about to embarrass Mark by telling her any details. It really wouldn't have helped any of us. My mother, although providing me with an excellent home, lacking for nothing including love and affection, was rather traditional in her thinking. Dad was a bit more broadminded, but would never go against her. So it was a case of what she didn't know wouldn't harm her.

"Although your father has arranged time off, you know what will probably happen." Dad was an inspector with the West Midlands Police Force. He would often be called in at short notice to deal with some emergency or other.

"I know. It happens too regularly. He ought to put his foot down."

"I've been telling him that for years, but you know your father."

The conversation dragged on as it usually did, with mum passing on bits of gossip, which frankly didn't interest me, but she thought I should know. At one point I turned to Mark and moved my fingers and thumb, imitating mum's constant talking. Mark cracked up, but managed to keep quiet.

Eventually the conversation died down, and I was able to terminate it without offending her. I had a few words with my dad, then we disconnected the call.

"Phew, she does go on a bit," I told Mark, collapsing on the couch beside him.

"I'm sure her heart is in the right place."

"Don't get me wrong. She's a good mother, but why she thinks I'd be interested in what next door's cat was getting up to on top of Dad's garage with the Tom from across the road I'll never know."

Mark chuckled.

"I get on okay with them, but I can't say we're truly close."

"That's a pity," Mark said, no doubt remembering his relationship with his dad and late mother.

"If I needed them, they'd be in the car heading back this way almost before the telephone receiver hit the cradle. We just don't have that much in common. I'll have to take you to see my gran sometime. She's got a flat in Leeds. She's a scream." I related the funnier aspects of my coming out to her. Mark found it hilarious.

"Tell you what," I said. "When we go over to see Gran, we'll take her to a gay pub."

Mark looked amazed. "Are you sure?"

"Well, if you'd feel uncomfortable about going into such a place, I understand, I've only been in a few, and it wasn't much fun on my own."

"No, no, it isn't that. I mean us taking your Gran."

I laughed, knowing full well what Mark was thinking. "She'd love it. She'd probably end up inviting a lesbian back to her flat."

"Wow, she seems like an amazing lady."

"She is. I used to spend most weekends at her house. I got drunk for the first time when I was with her. Mum and Dad were furious when they found out. Didn't bother Gran though. I'll tell you the whole story someday."

"Look forward to it."

"NO, DAD. PLEASE, no!"

Mark's shouting and thrashing about woke me instantly. I'd never seen anyone have a nightmare before, so I was acting on instinct. I turned on the bedside lamp at my side and reached for Mark. We had somehow separated in the night.

"Mark, Mark, love. It's Simon. You're having a bad dream. It's okay, you're safe now." I squeezed his shoulder. This seemed to rouse him. "It's okay. Just a bad dream, sweetheart."

"It was horrible."

"Did you dream about your dad?" I asked, pulling the still shaking young man into my arms.

He nodded.

"I don't know how you managed to stay with him." I rubbed his back and continued to make soothing noises.

"When Mum was dying she asked me to look after Dad once she'd gone. She knew we didn't really get on, but she thought we'd pull closer together after her death." Mark gave a hollow laugh. "That's the only reason why I stayed. I thought if I kept out of the old man's way, I could put up with living at home."

"I see." I knew talking about his home life wasn't easy, but I thought it better he get it all off his chest.

"I was dreaming about the day he found Danny and me in bed together. I'd never seen him so angry before. That's when he came out with all the hateful crap I told you about earlier."

I nodded.

"Dad pulled off his belt. Danny fled, and I cowered at the other side of my bed. When he lumbered round the room towards me, I leapt over the bed, and locked myself in the bathroom. He banged on the door for a bit, but he eventually went downstairs. I knew he'd soon drink himself into unconsciousness. So after a couple of hours I snuck out of the bathroom, got a few things together and left the house."

I kissed his cheek, encouraging him to continue.

"I went round to Danny's to see if he'd put me up for a while. He didn't want to get involved. He let me stop on his couch for a night, but I knew I'd have to leave the next day. At the bus station in Newcastle I counted up what bit of money I had, handed it over to the guy at the ticket office and asked him how far it would get me. Don't know if my question surprised him or not but he printed out a ticket for Littleborough, and here I am."

Mark seemed to sag once he'd told his story. I ran my fingers through his curls for a few minutes longer.

"I'm here for you. I'll do anything I can to help. I'm sure you know that by now," I whispered into the silence.

"Thank you. I do, and believe me, without you I…I…"

"It's okay." I kissed his lips briefly.

"I'm sorry about earlier…when I asked if we could have a tree. It's just…when those carol singers came round, I just wanted us to have a really nice Christmas. The last couple at home weren't very nice."

I kissed him again. "Silly man, we're going to have a tree, and loads of streamers and stuff around the house. We're going to have the best Christmas either of us can remember."

"Thanks, love," he said.

That was the first time I could ever remember Mark calling me love. This really wasn't such a revelation though, as here in the North it's a fairly commonly used word friends say to each other. But it sounded nice when Mark said it. I was determined to make this a very special Christmas for us both.

"And we're having turkey, and some of those little sausages with bacon wrapped around them, and as many types of stuffing as Marks & Spencer sells."

Mark sighed in happiness.

"We'll make it one to remember."

"Thanks."

"'S okay," I yawned. "Now we've got all that sorted, can we get back to the land of Nod?"

Mark and I snuggled together again, and allowed Morpheus to enfold us once again in his arms.

Chapter 7

"SORRY, MR SMITH, the nurse is running about half an hour behind schedule," the doctor's receptionist told Mark. "But if you take a seat, she will see you as soon as she can."

We found seats in the waiting room, crowded as usual with anxious mothers and their screaming, hyperactive children.

After a while I asked Mark if he'd be okay on his own for a bit. "I've just got a couple of errands I need to take care of."

Mark gave me a smile. "No problem."

"Thanks. I won't be long. Probably be back before you get seen."

"Okay, see you later."

I'd decided to get a surprise Christmas present for Mark. I hoped he wouldn't feel uncomfortable that he hadn't been able to get me a gift in return. Not one he could wrap anyway. Mark agreeing to spend Christmas with me would be gift enough.

I went into the local branch of Waterstones, the booksellers. I thought Mark would appreciate a book. I know: what would you expect a librarian to buy? They had a few copies of Dickens' *A Christmas Carol*. One in particular had a bright-red cover in tooled-leather. I thought he would like that. It was also small enough to fit in my pocket, so it wouldn't be difficult for me to get it home without Mark being aware of what I'd bought. I thought about writing an inscription in the book, but I couldn't put down on paper what I felt. Maybe I would think of something before I wrapped it.

My purchase made, I went back to the doctor's. Mark still hadn't been seen, so I waited with him. I read an ancient copy of the *Reader's Digest*, but felt guilty as Mark couldn't hold a book. He said he was okay staring at the posters on the wall extolling the virtues of giving up smoking, taking more exercise, and losing weight.

Finally his name was called. I asked him if he wanted me to go in with him and he agreed. I abandoned a 'fascinating' article on the problems of establishing rubber plantations in India in the early part of the century, and followed Mark into the treatment room.

"Now, Mr Smith, let's have a look at these dressings," the nurse, all businesslike, said. "And how have we been with them?"

"I don't know about you, nurse, but, for me, they've been itching a bit lately."

The nurse didn't appear to catch Mark's sarcasm.

"Good. The itching means your body is healing itself." She cut and unwrapped the bandages.

Mark's hands looked red to me, but the nurse seemed to think everything was healing nicely.

"That's it, you're done," she said once the new bandages were taped in place. "Make an appointment for the same time next week, and we'll see how they're doing then."

I remembered the sick note Mark would need to go with his benefit forms. The nurse said to ask the receptionist. We did, and she managed to collar a doctor, who after taking a quick glance at Mark's notes, gave him a certificate for a month. This was more than I thought he would get. The doctor saw my surprise and said if Mark found any work earlier, then the note could always be revised.

We left the surgery, I posted off the benefit forms, and we headed for Woolworth's to check out their decorations. I'd remembered to put the rucksack on Mark, as I thought we'd end up buying quite a bit.

We bought so much—despite Mark's protestations—I had to buy a second rucksack for myself. There was no way I could carry a plastic snowman as well, so we had to ditch that idea. Though I didn't give up hope altogether about buying one. Even so, we were a heavily laden pair who dragged ourselves through our front door.

"I don't know about you," I told Mark once I'd set down our bags, "but I need a cup of coffee."

"I wouldn't say no to a cup, either."

I went into the kitchen and put the kettle on. "You know, that isn't the end of the shopping," I told Mark, who was still in the living room.

I heard him groan. "Why, what have we forgotten?"

"Although we've plenty of food in, I want to get a few more special items. I want to make this a Christmas to remember!"

Mark had walked into the kitchen by this point and put his arms around me. "It already will be because you've agreed to share your home with me."

"Thanks." I swallowed. Originally I hadn't planned on doing much of a Christmas meal for just me. I'd bought a piece of turkey breast and a tiny foil-wrapped carton of stuffing. "I plan to do a large supermarket shop. I was going to walk up to Tesco, load myself up, and get a taxi back, but if you want to come, I don't mind. Otherwise I could ask Mary if she'd come round this evening and keep you company."

"I'll come with you. It doesn't seem fair to put Mary out."

"She won't mind. She'd enjoy spending the evening with a good looking man."

Mark blushed.

"Though on second thoughts, she did say she'd have her father's car for the early part of this week. I wonder if she'd take us to the supermarket? Believe me, that girl lives to shop. I swear her motto is 'When the going gets tough, the tough go shopping'."

Mark chuckled.

"Okay, then. Ring her up and see what she says."

"Going shopping with a couple of gay men, we'll have a whale of a time," was Mary's response over the phone when I asked for her help.

"Don't stereotype. Not all gay men enjoy shopping." I also asked her if she wanted to stay for the evening and have supper with us.

"I'd love to. Since Jerry left, I've just been pining away at home." She laughed.

"Yeah, right."

"Well, my honour couldn't be in danger with you two, could it?"

"I think you'll be safe with us. You can help decorate the house as well if you've a mind to. You know what I'm like up a step ladder."

"Course I'll help. Though you'd have thought a couple of gay men wouldn't need any help with decorating."

"Don't start all that again," I laughed.

"I'll come round about six. Be ready to shop, shop, shop!"

I groaned, said 'goodbye,' and hung up.

Going back into the kitchen, I related most of the conversation to Mark. "And if you think this morning's shopping expedition was tiring, just wait until you've seen Mary in action."

"I feel a headache coming on."

"Wimp."

❖

MARK AND I sat exhausted but very happy in the back of Mary's dad's car.

"Phew, I didn't think we'd ever get out of those shops alive!" Mark wiped his brow with his hand, then looked down, obviously forgetting his bandages.

"You men just don't have any staying power," Mary announced.

"I bet Jerry knew what he was doing when he took up that place on the field trip. If he could see us now he'd be laughing his socks off," I put in.

"Yeah," Mary admitted, "whenever I take him shopping, he hides in a record shop till I'm finished."

"Wise man," Mark said.

Mary looked in the rear view mirror and stuck out her tongue at Mark. We all laughed.

Pulling up in front of our house, we piled out of the car, and Mary and I carried in a frighteningly large amount of groceries: yet more decorations to add to the ones we'd bought earlier that day including an outdoor snowman and Father Christmas. I hadn't been able to decide which to get, so Mary had *persuaded* me to buy both.

"I'll go and put the kettle on. That'll give you two a chance to talk about me behind my back," I announced when all the groceries had been put away.

"What makes you think you're such an interesting topic of conversation anyway?" Mary asked.

"I'm deeply wounded." I mock limped to the kitchen.

This caused the other two to laugh. I got the drinks together on a tray and brought them back into the living room.

"Shhh, he's coming back in," Mary said as I entered.

"You see, you were talking about me."

"No, we just thought we'd wind you up a bit," Mark told me.

"It didn't work. After two rounds of shopping in one day,

I'm too knackered to be wound up."

"Yeah, thank god it's only once a year," Mark said. Though I noticed he said it with a wistful expression.

"You two. That was nothing! If I'd have had more time, I'd have driven you to Leeds, and then you'd have had something to complain about."

"Thank god for small mercies," I said.

Once we'd drunk our coffee, and recovered sufficiently, Operation Tinsel was put into effect. We trimmed the tree, including the angel which Mark had picked out. We had coloured paper streamers across the ceiling, white Christmas lights were pinned all around the front window, and I had managed to connect Father Christmas and the snowman to the electricity, placing them on either side of the front door.

Once everything had been done, I collapsed onto the couch between Mark and Mary. "Bloody hell, I'm totally bushed now."

"Well done." Mark put his arm around me and kissed me on the lips. I was a bit surprised he'd do this in front of Mary, but I was overjoyed that he did.

"Thanks." I kissed him back.

Mary cleared her throat.

"You still here? Um, I mean, would you like to stay for a bite of supper, or do you need to get home?"

She rolled her eyes, then looked over at the mantle clock. It was a little after ten. "I better go. Some of us have work in the morning."

"Aw, my heart bleeds. Just think of Mark and me cuddled up in bed tomorrow morning, enjoying a lie in, while you're battling your way to work."

"Lucky sods!"

"I know I'm very lucky," Mark said, staring into my eyes.

"Not as lucky as me," I whispered just before kissing him.

"Euw. You soppy sods," Mary said.

"You're just jealous," I told her.

"I am, I am," she said, getting up to leave. "I'll no doubt

see you two again before Thursday?"

"Yeah, probably." I managed to tear myself away from Mark's green eyes and perfect smile.

Putting her hand on the door knob, Mary said, "Behave yourselves."

"We'll try," Mark laughed.

"I'll see you to your car," I told Mary.

Mary unlocked her car door and looked at me.

"What?"

"You know that he loves you, don't you?"

I swallowed. "I hope so, because I've never loved anyone as much as I do him. I just can't tell him, in case you're...I'm wrong."

"Oh, Simon."

"I'd hate to think he felt he had to pretend to be in love with me just to stay."

"It'll all work out, you'll see." Mary gave me a hug.

I sighed. "Hope so."

"Speak to you again soon." She touched my cheek before getting behind the wheel.

I watched the tail lights disappear down the street, hoping Mary was right about Mark loving me.

Putting on a happy face, I walked back into the house.

"Now then," I said to Mark. "I prescribe a bite to eat, a bath, and then bed. Any objections?"

"None at all."

"I bought some muffins this evening. What do you say to toasting one on the fire and spreading it thickly with butter, so it'll run down your chin as it melts?"

"Sounds like heaven on earth."

We spent a wonderful evening sitting by the fire, toasting muffins, listening to Christmas music on the radio and enjoying each other's company.

Chapter 8

TUESDAY AND WEDNESDAY—the latter being Christmas Eve—flew by. We spent our time walking, talking, eating, sleeping, and cuddling. If it were possible, my love for Mark just grew and grew. More than once during those two days I found my mouth opening with the words 'I love you,' on the tip of my tongue. I always managed to stop myself just at the last second though. Imagine if Mark couldn't say the words back. That would certainly be the ideal recipe for a miserable Christmas. I knew I was facing a frustrating holiday, due to my reluctance...my fear...to be open and honest with Mark, but it would be off-set—in part—by ensuring Mark got a happy one. The last two he had faced hadn't been pleasant affairs. There was no way I was going to ruin this one for him.

Maybe I could tell him how I felt sometime in the New Year, if the right circumstances came up. I knew this was procrastination on my part. However, all my private sufferings would be worth it to see his happy, smiling face.

At about 6 o'clock on Christmas Eve the phone rang.

"Hello?"

"Hi, Simon," Mary said. "Mum and Dad are going to Midnight Mass at St John's. They were wondering if you and Mark would like to come along. We can pick you up and bring you back again."

"Erm. I don't know. Hang on a tick, I'll ask Mark." I turned to him and related what Mary had said.

"I'm not much of a churchgoer, but yes…yes I think I'd like to go if you would."

"Mary," I said into the phone, "we'd love to come."

"Great. We'll pick you up about ten-thirty."

"We'll be ready. And say thanks to your parents from us, will you?"

"Sure, see you later. Bye."

I hung up. "You sure you're all right about it?" I asked Mark.

He nodded. "It'll be nice to get back to the real meaning of Christmas. I like all the shopping and everything, but it's too easy to forget what it's really all about."

"Wow, that's deep."

"Sorry," Mark laughed.

THE TIME DREW near for Mary's parents to pick us up. Mark and I had gotten dressed in warm—but smart—clothing. Neither of us wore a tie. I had several, but as Mark didn't, I thought it'd be inappropriate for me to put one on.

Buttoning up Mark's coat, I said, "You never know how well those places are heated." I laughed apologetically. "Sorry, I must sound like your mother." Then I realised what I'd said.

"Oh, no! Sorry, Mark. What an insensitive thing to say."

"It's fine." He smiled. "In some very cute ways you act a bit like mum did. I like it."

I wasn't convinced.

"Simon, it's fine, honestly." He touched my cheek with his bandaged hand.

"I know I get a bit carried away with myself sometimes. Just give me a smack up the side of the head when it gets too much."

Mark laughed. "Well, any smacking will have to wait till these come off." He moved his bandaged hands higher.

"Shit, have I done it again?"

"No, no, not at all." He closed the distance between us and gave me a reassuring hug.

A few minutes later a car horn sounded. Looking out of the window I saw that it was Mary and her parents.

IT WAS A bit of a tight squeeze on the backseat of the car, but I wasn't about to complain about being pushed up against my best friend and the man I loved.

The service was great. We got to sing plenty of my favourite carols. The biggest surprise of the evening however, was Mark's voice. My god—whoops, shouldn't have thought that in church—but it, Mark's voice I mean, was beautiful. I shivered hearing it. I wondered if he had taken lessons.

The vicar centred his address on the phrase 'Peace on earth, goodwill to ALL men.' He seemed to put a stress on *all*. I'd no idea if he included gay men in that 'All', but I chose to believe he did and drew comfort from it.

Although communion was celebrated, neither Mark nor I had been confirmed so we didn't go up to receive it. That didn't seem to matter though, because there were lots of people who stayed in their pews, too.

The final carol was *Hark the Herald Angels Sing,* my absolute favourite. I raised up my totally out of tune voice. It felt so liberating to belt out such a triumphal hymn.

I thanked the vicar for his sermon and shook his offered hand just before leaving the church. I turned to see Mark give the cleric a salute with his bandaged right hand. In return the vicar patted Mark's shoulder.

When we got outside, we found to both Mark's and my delight it was gently snowing.

"A white Christmas, it couldn't be more perfect!" Mark said, blinking rapidly.

I pulled him to one side. "Would you rather we walk home? It isn't all that far."

"Could we?" He blinked some more.

I turned to Mary and her parents. I thanked them for the offer of a lift home, but told them of our decision to walk. After wishing them a Merry Christmas I watched them drive off.

Turning back to Mark I pulled him into a hug. We just stood there for the longest time, the snow softly falling on us. I could only recall one other white Christmas, and to be able to share this one with Mark was wonderful.

"Ready to go home now?" I eventually asked.

Mark nodded and let go of me.

"I don't remember them forecasting snow," I said as we started home.

"No, me neither."

"That all goes to prove how special it is then."

Mark was quiet for the rest of the journey home. I didn't want to interrupt his thoughts. I had some pretty wonderful ones going round in my own head.

"We're home," I said, locking the front door. "Would you like a cup of cocoa or something?"

"No, it's okay, thanks. If you'll just help me in the toilet and undress me, I think I'll turn in."

"Yes, of course."

Mark still seemed distracted. I didn't feel as though I ought to question him on it, so I did the things he asked.

I wasn't quite ready for sleep myself, so I told Mark I was going to make a hot drink, and would come to bed later.

I sat in front of the telly with my cup of cocoa. There was a discussion about the role of the church in modern society. It wasn't all that interesting, but it helped me to relax. Eventually I realised it was time I hit the sack. So I performed my ablutions and crawled beneath the sheets next to an already sleeping Mark. He was on his back, so I wasn't able to spoon in behind him. I lay still, excited about the happiness I hoped he'd find the next day. But eventually my thoughts settled and the sound of Mark's soft rhythmic snores gently lulled me into dreamland.

Chapter 9

I AWOKE BRIGHT and early on Christmas Day. Perhaps this was a throwback to my childhood, when I'd start nagging my parents about 6 am so I could go downstairs and see what Santa Claus had brought me. Mark still lay peacefully sleeping on his back. I looked down at his untroubled face: the gentle curve of his lips, the slight closing of his nostrils as he breathed in. I couldn't fathom why anyone could so much as think about hurting this angel. I don't know how long I stayed propped up on one elbow looking at the face of my love, framed as it was by his pillow and the duvet. Eventually his breathing changed, and he began to blink.

"Hello," he croaked.

"Merry Christmas."

"Same to you." He gave me a weak smile.

"Do you want to get up yet?"

He shrugged. "Might as well start the day."

As we went through our now familiar morning routine, I noticed that Mark seemed a bit distracted. I wondered if he was remembering the past two Christmases which hadn't been pleasant for him. I kept my concerns to myself, thinking the best thing would be to just be there for him if he needed to talk. Hopefully the happy events I'd planned for the day would bring him out of his melancholy.

"Would you like breakfast?" I asked when we'd gone downstairs, and I'd lit the fire.

"No, it's okay, I'm not that hungry."

"I plan to have Christmas dinner ready for about two o'clock, would that be okay?"

He shrugged. "Yeah, thanks."

I decided now was as good a time as any to give Mark his gift. I went into the kitchen and pulled out the wrapped book from the back of one of the cupboards.

"I know you couldn't get me a gift, but, because I wanted to make this year as special as I could, I got you a small something."

"I did get you a gift." He became animated for the first time that morning.

"Oh, how? I mean—"

"Mary helped me pick it and she wrapped it. It's at the back of that drawer." He pointed to a deep drawer under the video shelves. I put his gift on his knee while I went to retrieve mine.

"Wow, this is such a surprise," I said when I'd found the wrapped package and brought it back to the sofa where Mark was sitting. "Can I open mine first?" I asked in a child-like voice.

Mark smiled. "Of course."

It was a recording of Handel's *Messiah* I'd been wanting for a while now, but thought it a bit extravagant to spend so much money on myself. "Oh, Mark, it's great, how did you know I wanted this?"

"I asked Mary."

"Yes, of course. Thanks." I leaned over and kissed him on the lips. "Now, do you want me to open yours for you?"

"Please."

I unwrapped the book while it was still on his lap. "It's not very exciting, I'm not much good at picking out presents." I pulled back the paper to reveal the leather-bound volume. "I wrote something inside. I hope you like it." I lifted the cover to reveal the inscription so Mark could see.

My dearest Mark
I hope you can forget your own personal ghost of Christmas past.
Instead let's both think about our Christmases present and yet to come.
Simon, Christmas 1986

Mark stared at the book for the longest time. I saw his shoulders had started shaking. He was crying. What had I done wrong? Had I inadvertently made his memories of previous Christmases worse? He looked up at me and wiped his eyes on his bandages. He opened his mouth, but said nothing. He closed it again, swallowed and then began to speak.

"Simon, I'm sorry, but I can't hold this in any longer." He got up from the sofa and came and knelt down in front of me. He put his bandaged hands on top of mine. "Simon, please, please don't say anything until I've finished. Okay?"

I nodded while my mind began to frantically search for a reason for Mark being upset. Had I gone too far? Should I not have kissed him just now? What would I do if he said he wanted to find somewhere else to live? I felt tears threatening to fall.

"I want you, no, I need you to understand what I'm about to say, I mean from the bottom of my heart. I'm not saying it out of a sense of obligation. I mean it totally." He looked up at the ceiling. "Oh, God, this is so difficult." He then looked directly into my eyes. "Simon...I...I love you." He buried his head in my lap and wept.

I couldn't speak. My mind was turning cartwheels; did he say what I thought he'd said? It seemed that what I had wanted for so long had finally come to pass. He loved me, just as I loved him. Oh, joy of joys, sing hallelujah! I never thought another man, let alone one as beautiful both inside and out as Mark, would ever say those three magical words to me. I thought about the sincerity on his face and in his words. Yes, he truly meant what he'd said. I couldn't speak, but I could move. I rubbed his shoulders and then I stroked his hair.

Eventually I found my voice. "Mark, please look at me."

He slowly lifted his head.

"I love you, too. I've been too frightened to tell you. I never thought someone like me would ever, could ever, have someone as perfect or as awesome as you say they loved me."

"Why not?" he asked through his still falling tears.

"Because, sweet Mark, I'm not attractive. I'm plain. The rare times I tried to find someone…" I shook my head, not wanting to think about all that now. "…well, let's just say it didn't work. I just ended up being hurt."

"In everything that matters to me you're beautiful. I've always believed it's what's in someone's heart that counts. And you've got a good heart, a beautiful heart."

The dam of tears finally burst; no one had ever said such kind and tender things to me before. I'd felt for a long time it was what a person was like on the inside that mattered the most. I never thought I'd find someone else who felt the same way, but this truly wonderful man kneeling in front of me did.

Mark got up from his kneeling position and sat beside me. We remained on the sofa for what seemed like hours, no one was watching the clock. We kissed, we hugged and we cried some more.

Eventually I spoke. "I'm so glad you told me. I don't think I'd have ever had the courage to say anything. I didn't want to spoil another Christmas for you. Imagine if you didn't feel the same as me? You might have felt that you'd have to pretend to love me to stay here. I couldn't put you through that."

"You see, that's what I meant by you being beautiful on the inside. You always put my happiness before your own. It takes a special person to do that. It's just one of the many reasons why I love you so much."

"Oh, Mark." I kissed him.

"Last night, when we came out of the church, and I saw we were going to have a white Christmas, I thought it was like a sign or something. But I hesitated. I mean, I've not come from the best of backgrounds, and I thought maybe you didn't feel the same way about me. But, I don't know, it was the book. The straw that broke the camel's back if you like. I felt that maybe you might love me too. I just couldn't go on any longer without telling you."

"I'm so glad you did. It was killing me not being able to tell you how I felt."

We kissed a little more, but mostly we just held each other, Mark lying between my legs, his back against my belly and chest.

Stroking Mark's curls, I said, "I first realised I loved you when I found you lying in that hospital bed. You were asleep. I looked down at you, and it was like something had slammed into me. I just knew I had to love you. Even if you couldn't love me back, I thought that just me loving you would be enough. I didn't realise how painful that would be though."

"I'm sorry."

"Silly man." I kissed the top of his head. He had nothing to apologise for. "It's like a huge weight has been lifted from my shoulders. You'll have to keep holding on to me for a while, because if you don't I think I might float away."

Mark turned until we were chest to chest. Putting his arms around me, he said, "I'll hold you for as long as you need me to."

Time passed as we held on to each other, neither of us wanting to separate.

Eventually I said, "If I don't put the turkey on soon, we

won't be eating till Boxing Day."

I felt Mark's chuckle against my chest. "You asked me a while back, it seems like a lifetime ago now, if I was hungry. I am now. Do you think we could have something to eat?"

"Coming right up, angel."

We moved to the kitchen together, neither of us wanting to break the contact. We laughed at our silliness.

"Will toast do you? It'll take me a while to get dinner ready."

"Toast will be great."

So I put a couple of rounds of toast through the toaster, spreading each as soon as it popped up with butter and marmalade, feeding my man as we stood at the worktop together. We still held onto each other throughout all of this.

When we finished, I wiped his mouth with a paper towel, kissed him on the lips and said, "I can taste Seville oranges."

"So can I."

"When those bandages come off, will you still let me feed you sometimes?"

"Only if you'll let me feed you, too," Mark said.

"Deal."

We kissed some more, the exchanges becoming increasingly passionate.

Eventually—and with reluctance—I withdrew. "Listen, love, I need to get on with dinner. Although I don't want to let go of you, it'll be a bit awkward if I don't."

"Oh," Mark sighed dramatically. "I'm being passed over for a twelve-pound turkey."

We both cracked up. Mark went and sat on his stool. All through the meal preparation, I couldn't last for more than a few minutes without going back to touch or kiss him. Maybe I just needed the reassurance he was still real…still in love with me.

Because of the earlier delays, we would eat about an hour or so later than I'd planned. We found we had enough time to go into the living room and watch the Queen's speech before eating. I can't remember anything she said. It was probably the usual bland platitudes that had been recycled from previous years. Don't misunderstand, I'm all for the royal family, but I could never get too worked up about the Christmas address to the nation and Commonwealth.

Soon after the national anthem finished, the meal was ready to serve.

"I've got another surprise for you," I said to Mark.

"Oh?"

"Yeah." I reached up to the top shelf of the main cupboard and brought down a box of Christmas crackers.

"I love pulling crackers," Mark said with enthusiasm. Then he looked at his bandages.

"No, I've worked that one out," I told him before he could get too upset. I got down on my knees and took off his right shoe and sock.

"What are you doing?"

"You can't use your hands, so you'll have to use your toes." I lifted his foot slightly and fitted a cracker between his big toe and the next one. I held the other end of the cracker in my hand.

"Now pull downwards with your foot," I said.

Amazingly it worked. I got out the plastic novelty, a set of false teeth, read the stupid and totally un-funny motto, and put the coloured paper hat on Marks head.

"You look daft," I told him.

He laughed. "We'll have to pull yours now, and you have to use your foot, too."

I took off my left shoe and sock, and put another cracker on the floor between us. I slid the thin part of the cracker between our toes and pulled. I got a comb in my cracker, quite useful I thought. The motto was just as lame as Mark's, though.

"Aren't you going to put on the hat?" Mark asked.

"Nah, I look silly in them."

"If I'm going to look silly, so are you."

I couldn't argue with his logic, so I put a hat on, too. This caused much mirth from my boyfriend.

Wow, Mark is my boyfriend, the thought only just occurring to me.

"You know," Mark said, "in future years, I'm going to insist we always pull our crackers this way."

"Not if we have company," I said.

"Rubbish, it'll be a scream. We might even start a trend."

We both laughed while I put our shoes and socks back on.

"Anyway, the dinner's ready now," I said, getting up from the floor.

We had decided not to have a starter as the turkey, two kinds of stuffing, cranberry jelly, chipolata sausages, mashed potatoes, Brussels sprouts, carrots and gravy, with Christmas pudding and brandy butter to follow, was quite sufficient.

To say we were stuffed after eating that lot would be a gross understatement.

"I don't think I can move," Mark shifted on his stool.

"Me neither. Oh, bugger the washing up. I'll do it later," I said.

Mark laughed, groaned, then brought his bandaged hands to his belly. "Don't. It's too painful."

We did manage to move, but only as far as the sofa.

"Are you enjoying the day so far, love?"

Mark looked at me, a huge smile on his face. "It's been the best Christmas ever. Because I've got the best present I could ever have wished for."

I looked at him quizzically.

His response consisted of a single word. "You!"

I gave him the biggest, wettest kiss I could. "Thanks, angel. That means the world to me."

We settled back against each other.

"All that food has made me sleepy," Mark said.

"So sleep."

"I don't think I could make it upstairs."

"Sleep here."

Mark stretched out on the sofa with his head in my lap. He fell asleep with his face pointing towards me. I couldn't help gazing once again into my boyfriend's face. He'd had such a troubled past couple of years. It amazed me he was still the kind, sweet and trusting person he was. If I'd gone through what he had, I think I'd have ended up being bitter and cynical.

I gently ran my index finger along the bridge of his nose and traced along the line of his lips. I couldn't help shedding a silent tear of joy that somehow I'd miraculously captured the heart of this angel.

The ringing of the phone shattered the silence of the room. Mark jerked awake. I was a bit annoyed that the outside world had intruded on our little piece of heaven.

I got up; the muscles in my legs had grown stiff from being in the same position for an extended period. I stretched them backwards slightly to work out the stiffness.

"Hello?"

"Simon, sorry to bother you on Christmas Day, but I just couldn't wait any longer to find out if you two were having a good time."

"Hi, Mary. Mark and I were just relaxing after overeating at dinner."

"Sorry I've disturbed you."

"Anyone else and I'd be upset, but I'm so glad to talk to you. Hang on a sec." I covered the mouthpiece and asked Mark if I could tell her our news.

Mark smiled, got up from the sofa and approached. "We'll tell her together."

We agreed on a form of words, and I uncovered the mouthpiece. "Mary, Mark and I have something to tell you."

"Oh?"

I held the phone between us, and we both said, "We love each other."

I had to move the phone away as Mary's screeches of joy would have burst our eardrums.

Once Mary's excitement had died down, she said, "When did you tell each other? No, on second thoughts I'm inviting myself round. You can feed me later, too."

"Cheeky madam," I said. "Is it okay to leave your family today of all days?"

"God, yes. Auntie Margaret and Uncle Jim are snoring their heads off in front of the telly, and Mum and Dad look like they'll be joining them soon."

I laughed. "Okay then. The roads aren't too dangerous with the snow are they?"

"No, we only got a light dusting. Haven't you been out today?"

"We were too busy with other things," Mark said.

We all laughed.

"I'll see you in a few minutes," I told her.

"Get the sherry out."

"We will," Mark said.

We said goodbye and I hung up.

AS PROMISED, MARY arrived within ten minutes. Once inside she held us both in a three-way hug.

"Thank heavens both of you have found each other at last."

"We've been living together for less than a week!" Mark protested.

"Yes, but you've known each other for months. When Simon here told me about when you two first met, well, I have to say, I was a bit shocked. But it couldn't have worked out better for you two."

We both thanked her.

"I'm sorry, Mark, about your hands, but do you think you'd have got together as soon if it wasn't for the accident?"

"No, I think you're right, we wouldn't," he admitted.

"Well, just goes to show, every cloud has a silver lining."

"And what a lining," I said as I embraced Mark.

"You can stop all that now I'm here." Mary wagged her finger at us.

"Sod off, I've only just found him. I have to touch him at

least every five minutes just to make sure he's still mine," I said.

"God help us," Mary said, rolling her eyes.

"Let us cast our minds back," I began. "We were eating hamburgers after going to the cinema—"

"All right, all right, but I'm sitting on the couch between you two lovebirds. I'm going to soak up a bit of your love, and hopefully it'll last me until Jerry gets back."

"Aw. Are we missing our man?" Mark asked as we sat as Mary had directed.

"Yes we are. He managed to ring this afternoon. Goodness knows how much those calls are costing him, but it was great to hear his voice."

"Get the violin out, Mark," I said. "Ouch!" Mary had hit me.

"Serves you right," Mark and Mary said together. We all laughed.

"Are you sure you two aren't related?" I asked.

"Daft sod." Mary shook her head. "Anyway, some hosts you two are. I've been here at least five minutes, and I haven't been offered a drink yet."

"Don't look at me. No hands," Mark said, lifting his arms.

"Between you two, I've really got my work cut out, haven't I?" I asked.

"Yes," they chorused.

I rolled my eyes, and walked toward the kitchen. Remembering Mark hadn't asked for any painkillers today I asked if he would join us in having sherry.

"Yes, I'll just have a small one. It's Christmas after all."

I smiled and entered the kitchen. Popping my head back around the door I told Mary, "You're only having a small one, too 'cause you're driving," I reached for the bottle of sherry.

"Unless you want to sleep with us," I heard Mark say.

"She's having a small one," I called out. With feeling I continued, "I'm the only one you're ever going to sleep with from now on, mister!"

"Damned right," I heard Mark say.

Leaving the sherry, I came back into the living room, walked back to Mark and knelt by him on the sofa, put my arms around him and kissed him tenderly on the lips.

"Oh, you two," Mary said. Mark and I kissed for another 30 seconds or so, then Mary piped up, "Am I ever going to get that bloody drink?"

"Sorry," I said.

I went back into the kitchen and soon returned with three sherries and gave one to Mary. "You'll have to budge up. I'm going to give my man his drink."

"No, I'll do it," she said.

"Okay then." I gave her the second glass.

I must admit, she made a pretty good job of giving Mark the drink. I thought about using a straw and putting the glass on the table, but a sherry glass is so small, and I thought it would be nicer for him to drink out of a glass for a change.

"Any idea when those bandages can come off?" she asked.

"The nurse is having a look on Monday. Might be lucky then," Mark said.

"Fingers crossed," I said.

"Not with these on!" Mark said, holding up his hands.

We chatted for a while, until the phone rang.

"Hello?" I said into the instrument.

"Merry Christmas."

"Gran! Merry Christmas to you, too."

"How's my favourite grandson?"

I smiled into the receiver. "You've only got the one grandson, and he's the happiest man in the world."

"I ought to call more often if I have such a strong effect on you."

I laughed. "How are you and the old ladies?" Gran always called the other residents of the bungalows and flats around her the 'old ladies,' even though quite a number of them were younger than she was.

"They're all fine. Mrs Draper at number twenty-six didn't

want to come to the lunch at the centre, but I told her she was going and I banged on her door till she came out."

Gran was the unofficial social secretary of their little community. She would organise trips to the seaside during the summer and parties at Christmas, New Year, and any other time she could persuade the other residents to let their hair down.

"Now, tell your old Gran what's got you so happy this Christmas. Did Father Christmas put something nice in your stocking?"

"Very nice." I put my hand over the mouthpiece and told Mark who was calling. "Can I tell her about us?"

He nodded.

"Gran, me again, sorry for that." I let out a breath. "I'm in love with the most perfect man."

I could see Mary rolling her eyes, and Mark hid his face.

"That's wonderful!"

"Yes." I couldn't help my silly grin. "I knew I was in love with him last week, and we told each other this morning as we unwrapped our presents."

"Wonderful. What's his name? I want to talk to him."

"Mark. He's called Mark. Just a second." I covered the mouthpiece. "Mark, Gran would like a word with you. I deliberately took my hand away from the mouthpiece. "Don't be embarrassed by what she tells you. The old girl's got a mind like a sewer!"

I could hear her protests, even though the receiver wasn't next to my ear. When she quieted, I held the phone against Mark's ear.

"Hello Mrs err, sorry, Gran…Yes…Yes…Really?…He didn't!…No." He laughed, then became serious. "Yes, Gran, I love him. With all my heart. I know, he's very precious to me, too."

There was a long pause as Gran told him something.

"Yes, he told me about him coming out to you…I laughed when he told me."

Gran talked for about a minute.

"No, I'm the lucky one...I hurt my hands, and they're in bandages. Simon has done everything for me, and he hasn't complained once...Yes, everything." Mark reddened at this point.

I knew what she'd just asked.

"It's been nice talking to you, too, Gran. I'm looking forward to meeting you, too. Yes. I'll put him on."

I moved the phone back to my ear. "Have you been embarrassing my boyfriend?" I couldn't believe how wonderful it was to say the words 'my boyfriend' to another person.

"Would I?" Gran asked.

"Do you really want me to answer that?"

Gran laughed. "He sounds like a very nice young man. You'll have to bring him down to see me in the New Year."

"Yes, Gran, I will. Believe me, I want to show him off." I looked at Mark, and he went red again. "I'll let you go. No doubt you're planning to bully some more defenceless old ladies into another knee's up."

"How did you guess?"

We laughed, then said our goodbyes and hung up.

"She's wonderful," Mark said.

"Yeah, she's pretty special," I admitted.

"I've never met anyone so full of beans," Mary smiled.

We chatted for a while longer, then Mary asked Mark, "So, what did Simon get you for Christmas?"

"A book."

Mary laughed. "Bloody typical. I swear, he eats, drinks, and breathes books."

"No, honestly, it's perfect. Would you show it to Mary?" Mark asked me.

I passed the book to her.

She read the inscription. "Aw, nice. Simon, why don't you read something from it?"

I took the book and leafed through it for a while, then began to read aloud:

'You'll want all day to-morrow, I suppose?' said Scrooge.

'If quite convenient, sir.'

'It's not convenient,' said Scrooge, 'and it's not fair. If I was to stop half-a-crown for it, you'd think yourself ill-used, I'll be bound?'

The clerk smiled faintly.

'And yet,' said Scrooge, 'you don't think me ill-used, when I pay a day's wages for no work.'

The clerk observed that it was only once a year.

Mary laughed. "Sounds just like our bosses at the Town Hall."

All three of us looked through the book and read out passages. Mary turned the pages for Mark.

After about an hour, she asked, "Am I going to get fed here or what?"

"Are you actually hungry? I'd have thought you'd have stuffed yourself at dinner?"

"I did, but I've got a couple of empty corners now."

"Would you like something, angel?" I knew my gaze was besotted, but I didn't care.

"Just a little, please."

"Turkey sandwiches?" I asked the pair.

Both agreed.

"WELL, I HOPE you like turkey, Mark, because you'll be having it for days yet," I said as I emerged from the kitchen, a tray of sandwiches in hand.

Mary laughed. "It'll be just the same at our place."

"I'll freeze some tonight, so we won't have as much to face in one go."

"Good idea," Mark said.

A short while later Mary announced she had to go. "Mum and I are going into Leeds tomorrow for the Boxing Day sales.

Want to come?"

"Hell, no!" Mark and I exclaimed.

"I've seen enough shops for at least a month," I said.

"Me, too," Mark added.

"You two! You don't know what you're missing."

"We do: endless queuing, pushing and shoving, not to mention the bruises when you get between someone and the bargain of the century," Mark said.

"You're both wimps."

"I don't care. Mark and I are going to spend the day together quietly. We might go for a walk if the weather's decent."

"Just like an old married couple," Mary sighed.

"What's wrong with that?" Mark asked.

"Absolutely nothing."

"Anyway, be gone woman. I want to make love with my man here." I put my arm around a reddening Mark.

A surprised Mary said, "I'm definitely going now." She headed for the door.

"See you soon," I called out after her.

Once she'd gone, and I'd locked the door, Mark said, "Do you really want to make love with me?"

"Yes, but…" I couldn't meet his gaze. The happiness of a few moments earlier had been replaced with trepidation. "I've never done it before," I added quietly.

Mark hugged me, then kissed me. "It's okay. We'll take it slow. I want your first time to be perfect."

"With you, my angel, it couldn't be anything else." I put my arm around his waist and we climbed the stairs together.

About the Author

HAVING READ ALL the decent free fiction on the net Drew could find, he set out to try his hand at writing something himself. Fed up reading about characters who were super-wealthy, impossibly handsome, and incredibly well-endowed, Drew determined to make his characters real and believable.

Drew lives a quiet life in the north of England with his cat. Someday he hopes to meet the kind of man he writes about.

CPSIA information can be obtained at www.ICGtesting.com
Printed in the USA
236196LV00009B/122/P